VISIONS OF A
LOTUS FLOWER

GEM

Visions of a Lotus Flower, Vol. 1

GEM

Cover art by saika

Chapter art by Keiko Nakamura

Visions of a Lotus Flower Vol. 1

Get in Touch:

instagram.com/gempublishing | gempublishing2@gmail.com

instagram.com/keiko.h.art

instagram.com/saika_illust | saika.work8@gmail.com

ISBNs: 979-8-8196-8855-7 (paperback)

10 9 8 7 6 5 4 3 2 1

First Edition

Printed in the United States of America

Contents

Chapter 1A

Chapter 1A:
The Drought

The world set ablaze; this is how I envision it. Not in a physical sense, but I imagine a world where utter chaos breaks out. When hearing that, many things may come to mind. War, death, and disease may be a few, but there are countless other things we've been conditioned to think of when we hear "utter chaos." Such stories are as old as humanity itself. However, the chaos I imagine is something completely different. What I'm thinking of is a world where people are free of masks; free to speak their own opinion on anything they want without fearing any sort of negative consequence that would arise from this openness. At first, this doesn't seem like a bad thing to desire; a world where people are freed of the societal shackles that bind us, but this becomes an impossibility when thinking about what would occur from this. War would be rampant, fear would be at an all-time high, and despite this honesty that I dream of - no one would trust one another. I fear that, without this common facade shared amongst us, the world would no longer be somewhere people would feel safe. For those reasons alone I would describe my dream as "utter chaos."

On another note, fire is commonly associated with the start of humanity; rather, humans being able to harness fire. Seeing as how chaos and fire go hand-in-hand, I wonder if humans were destined to destroy themselves. Although the idea of destiny is something that I frown upon, I can't help but wonder.

To backtrack, wanting such chaos is an extremely privileged viewpoint that I'm aware of and have taken into consideration. Either way, let me cut straight to the main issue at hand - we are in a period of drought. A period of stagnation where nothing exciting will ever happen. That is, of course, because humans are reaching a point technologically where any conflict is without a doubt mutually assured destruction. I do not want to cause conflict; I simply want to plant a few seeds of doubt in people's minds. Seeds that remind people not to be complacent, not to take things for granted, and remind people how dearly they all cling on to the hundreds of perfectly constructed strings that puppet us around every single day. However, even though these strings are perfectly constructed, they are only strings.

○

It was 4:00 pm and I was sitting on the bridge by the school waiting for Asa and Ayama as I usually do. I don't go to school that often anymore. I know it's a cliché for someone like me not to go, but I truly do not find value in it. One might argue that sitting on a bridge has equally as little value… and I'd have nothing more to add to that.

The bridge I frequent isn't directly near the school, but it's part of a larger complex of walking paths in the surrounding area. Asa and Ayama need to use the bridge to get home, so this is the perfect spot to wait. Anyways, seeing as how it's a popular trail, passersby are common. Although mostly the same people walk here every day. At around 4:00 pm, a young couple walks by. They've been on this conquest of disrupting my sacred 4:00 pm peace for a couple of months now.

I bring a book so I don't look odd to the passerby, but I've brought the same book for as long as the school year has been going on. This is important because there is only a week left of school. Bringing a book for the sole purpose of looking normal, despite the fact that reading the same book for months probably looks equally as odd is a bit redundant, but as I said, there's only a week of school left, so I might as well stick with it. To go back to the couple, I can tell her feelings are fading. Every day, the spark is a little less bright.

As she walked past me, her head was facing down and not at her partner.

Will she tell him how she truly feels, or will she wait until he notices? I could speculate, but interpersonal relationships aren't my strong suit, intrapersonal relationships are much more interesting to me. However, the line between the two is vague. Sometimes it's hard to decipher what falls into either category. I wouldn't say I'm a people person, so maybe I'm wrong about the 'spark', but I know how to navigate conversations to the point where someone could mistake me for being one. This is not arrogant of me to say, I'm simply confident in my skills.

Tomorrow, maybe I'll go up to him and say, "Hey! She doesn't care about you! She much prefers looking at the ground than she does looking at you!"

"Yo! Owari!" someone called out in the distance.

Did I say that out loud?!

I picked my head up from the book and glanced in the direction the shouting was coming from, expecting the man to scold me…but it was just Asa.

"Even after all this time, it still amazes me how you can get louder each subsequent day," I said while closing my book and laying it on the bench space next to me.

"You know what, since we're being honest Owari, it still amazes me how you think you're spending your time wisely by sitting on this bench waiting for us instead of going to school."

I have nothing more to add to that.

Asa was standing in front of Ayama, so I looked past him and tilted my head so I could see her. "Hey Ayama, how was your day? You guys were a little later than usual," I said, still tilting my head.

"We have final exams, so we had to stay a little longer to finish the test."

"Ehm, YOU had to stay a little longer to finish the test. I was the first to finish as a matter of fact!" Asa triumphantly announced, marching forward a few feet while flaunting his arms to then turn back to Ayama.

"You wouldn't have left without me, Asa..."

"I know, I know. I'm only kidding~"

I picked up my book off the bench and got up to walk with them. Asa always walks faster than Ayama, but I stay behind with Ayama most days. Asa doesn't walk *too* far ahead, but it's usually a cycle of him walking ahead, stopping, waiting, then walking ahead again, then stopping, then walking again. Asa isn't the athletic type per se, just very energetic.

The path we take connects to most parts of the town. Some parts are vibrant and filled with nature, other parts are gray and cold. Lucky for us, the three of us live outside the town center so we're able to walk in the nature-filled parts. It's about a twenty-minute walk to get home. That being said, we live in a hilly area, so it's quite the walk - but the weather was nice today.

"You said you finished the test first, right Asa?" I asked.

"Of course."

"What *did* you get on it anyway?" Ayama curiously asked. She asked like she had no idea, but I was fairly certain she knew a rough estimation.

"Well, I got sixty."

"A sixty..." I replied in a condescending tone.

"Hey! Sixty is average! And you know what, scoring sixty percent means that I mastered over half of the topics that we learned over the year!"

"It also means that you were clueless about forty percent of the topics."

"In Asa's defense, Owari, this is our final year and it's not like we need an above-average grade to advance our academic career."

"Thank you, Ayama! I appreciate that!"

"Are you sure you're not just saying that because you got a good grade on the test?"

"While that may be the case," she paused and sidelong glanced at Asa, "don't say it in front of him!" Ayama whispered loudly while bursting into covert laughter.

"What?? You got a good grade on the test??" Asa exclaimed as his jaw dropped.

"Why do you think I stayed after for a little longer, dummy?"

"I guess you're right," Asa said in a disheartened tone. He continued directly after, immediately switching his vocal inflection like he forgot what we were originally talking about. "Oh, but Owari! You may be flaming me for getting an average score, but you got a zero percent!"

"Although that may be true from your perspective, what you don't know is that I actually take online classes on my phone and that's what I've been doing while waiting for you both every day!"

"What?? You do??" Asa asked, elongating his speech.

"No. But wouldn't that be quite the turn of events?"

"Shut up."

We all laughed, albeit some of us a little more than others, and continued on our journey through the windy path that led to our homes. We were on an upwards hill, so it was Asa's time to enact his trademarked 'Rush to The Top and Wait' technique. Very effective if I might add. If anything though, it gave me a chance to talk with Ayama without Asa interrupting.

"So…what *did* you get on the test?"

"One hundred."

I hid my laugh with my hand.

"Whatt? Why're you laughing…"

"I'm laughing at Asa. He thinks you got a good grade

obviously, but I don't think he knows it's *that* good."

"Haha yeah…but you, if anyone, should know that stuff like that doesn't really matter.." she tenderly replied.

My fixed gaze at Ayama broke when Asa started yelling. "What are you laughing about over there Owari?!"

And he still interrupts us! How did he even see me laugh? I don't like to raise my voice, so I usually wait till I get to the top to give him an answer in situations like this, but I didn't.

We continued talking on the downhill and Asa brought up the idea of us buying bicycles to get home faster after school, but Ayama said she enjoyed walking home. She said it was one of the only times that all three of us talked as a group. I didn't attend school for one, but two because I had to take care of my dad when I got home. Both of which are true, but I felt bad because I could eliminate one if I wanted to. On the contrary, spending a finite amount of time with someone makes the interaction a lot more meaningful, so I don't mind.

○

Asa is quite straightforward but also misleading. On one hand,

I'd say he's average in most places. Average grades, average appearance, average dreams, etc. He's smart and capable but doesn't apply himself too often. On the other hand, he's not as shallow of a person as you'd see in TV dramas, like the class clown who uses humor to hide their insecurities or the clueless one who gets by through sheer dumb luck, but he's not as complex as some others, at least on the surface. He has more to him, obviously, but I'm not going to probe him for information. He chooses not to share that side of him, so I must respect his choice. But as a friend, it's important to let him know the option is there. It's easy to hide large parts of your personality by simply being annoying and loud (he abuses that fact heavily). Intentional or not, that's how it is. I'm surprised I've been able to be friends with Asa seeing as how he only shows snippets of his personality... I mean, I do mean it when I say that I'd prefer someone to drop their social mask around the people that care about them, but I also fall victim to it, so I can't be upset to the point where I don't associate myself with anyone. I enjoy having friends. It's nice to interact with people you enjoy being around, as obvious and mundane as that might sound.

I do think that Ayama is mainly honest in the way she

acts though. She's timid, smart, and thoughtful. She's not uptight, she knows when to let loose and joke around, but I can tell she gets tired easily. Not tired as in physically exhausted, but her social battery runs out faster than mine or Asa's does. She opens up to me sometimes, but from my point of view, they're all pretty trivial matters. Not to belittle what she is going through, but it's all just… normal problems that people around our age go through. It's a fair assumption to say that she and Asa have pretty good lives.

Something that's been a passing thought of mine is how the world would be like if people's so-called 'social masks' were to be broken. However, it is nothing but a thought.

○

The paths we walk through are just dirt, so our shoes were fairly dirty. Not that we mind too much to the point where we'd take a bus home or something, because we all prepare accordingly and wear shoes that we wouldn't mind if they got messed up. I'd be lying if I said it wasn't a slight annoyance though. I looked down at my black shoes then looked at Ayama's and Asa's. Ayama's and mine were equally as dirty, but Asa's were sparkly clean. I had so many questions, but I let it be.

Walking for a couple more minutes, we got to where Asa splits off onto a diverging path to head home. Most days, we usually stop at the intersection to talk for a little bit.

I closed my eyes. I could hear birds chiming, I could feel the slight breeze brush up against my skin, and the consistent sound of water flowing laid my mind to rest…it truly was a beautiful day. For a brief moment, I was at peace. The kind of peace where I could've laid down and stared at the sky for hours without becoming bored.

"Yo. Owari."

As I said, just for a brief moment.

"Yes, Asa?" I said with my eyes still closed.

"Are you going to be a monk now?"

"Orange doesn't suit me," I said as I opened my eyes and looked at him with slight disdain.

He stuck his tongue out in retaliation then did a dramatic pose as though he were the main actor in a play written by Shakespeare. "So I guess this is where we part ways…" He said as he shoved his face into his elbow and nuzzled Ayama's shoulder, starting to make fake crying sounds. "Bye..guys…" he added, sniffing.

Ayama was playing along, so she grabbed his two shoulders and looked him in the eyes in a serious manner. "It'll be alright, Asa. We'll see each other in the morning, okay?"

"Okay…" He looked down with disappointment. After a few seconds, he switched back to his normal energetic self. "Welp! Ok then. See y'all tomorrow!"

"Bye Asa…" we said in unison.

After Asa left onto the diverging path, we continued walking along the main path to our homes. My house was technically closer to Asa's than Ayama's, so you'd normally assume Ayama would be the last one to get home, but I walked her home every day to make sure she got there safely.

"Bye Owari, I'll see you at school tomorrow~"

She knows that I won't come to school even though she tells me that everyday, but it's endearing nonetheless. I'm glad I'm friends with the two of them.

I started walking back home and got there after about five minutes. Taking my dirt-covered shoes off and placing them next to the door, I knocked twice as I opened it. "I'm home!"

There was no response, but the TV was blasting. The program that was on was a game show of some sort; an obnoxious one where people answered trivia facts that no normal person would know. I searched for the remote and turned it off. Once I did, the room turned black and it was hard to see in front of me, so I turned on one of the lamps that just barely lit the room. I wondered who turned on the TV in the first place. Now that the TV was off though, I walked through the living room to my dad's bedroom - one of two bedrooms in the house. The lights were off, but he was awake mumbling incoherent sounds under his breath. He had towels on his head and moved from what looked like discomfort in the position he was laying in every couple of seconds.

I walked back through the living area and moved to the kitchen to grab some of his medicine and a bottle of water; going back to his room to give it to him. He never spoke once...but he never does.

I waited there for fifteen minutes making sure his fever went down and removed the towels from his forehead. "Make sure you're drinking your water," I said as I sat him in an upright position. "I'm heading out."

He dully moved his head up and down to show his acknowledgment and I walked out the door, once again putting on my dirty shoes.

I was on the street now, and the sun was setting after only about twenty minutes of walking. The sun was hidden behind the mountains now, so the only thing keeping me from being blind was the seldom streetlights. I don't necessarily have a destination when I walk, I mainly do it since I don't find it particularly engaging to be at home. Walking with no direction is a good way to lose track of time; I didn't even notice that the natural dirt paths had turned into the lifeless gray.

I brushed past a woman who was frantically running to where I was coming from. I was imagining a murderer of some kind chasing her down the eerily empty street…but that murderer never came. Things like that are the reasons I don't like cities; they always feel so unsafe.

I sought refuge from the city by sitting on a bench by the lakefront. The birds were now asleep, and the cool breeze turned into a sharp cold front; there was no sound of water. My efforts for comfort were slightly unfruitful, but I did feel safer here. Unraveling my headphones was a pain, but I like city pop enough to make the effort. Before I knew it though, I was back at home and he was asleep. I sighed a breath of relief and went to sleep myself.

Will the rest of my life be the same as this?

Interlude 1

I am falling. Falling in a dark void... Continuously... without
an end in sight. It feels like I can see infinitely far, but it also
feels like I can't see more than an inch ahead. All my sense of
depth was lost. Wait... Asa and Ayama are here! But they fall
faster than me while I seemingly stay in place. Perhaps they
are going to -

...

     I saw a figure spreading its arms as flashes of colors
extend from its arms like wings. I reached my hand out and
tried to crawl closer, but I couldn't reach. The figure appeared
in a god-like pose. It wasn't reaching its arms out to me, but it

did seem like it wanted me to come closer. I strained every muscle in my body to reach the figure. I found that I was holding my breath while trying to move toward it, so once I noticed, I started breathing again. As I resumed breathing, I involuntarily gave up on trying to move forward. I stopped and the figure transformed into a lanky, devilish creature and contorted in unnatural ways as if taunting me for giving up.

…

It disappears.

…

Once again, I'm in a blank void with nothing in sight. No Asa or Ayama, no figure, nothing. I laid there for what seemed like hours trying to comprehend what I had just seen… and what was happening in general. As I looked back in my memory to try and decipher what that figure was, it all seemed so foreign. I was starting to doubt if it even happened.

…

Suddenly, I see something in the distance fall at a rapid speed. I first saw it appear when it was at eye level and watched it drop for about four seconds before it disappeared into the abyss below me. Since I only saw it for a split second, I wasn't able to figure out what exactly it was. Almost immediately after that, bodies that were void of character fell in rapid succession. They couldn't be regular bodies, they resembled mannequin-like figures. There are hundreds - no, thousands.

Without warning, I started falling in tandem with the bodies and I could feel something pushing me down.

…

…

…

I jolted up and started breathing heavily.

I regret not going to school,

I regret not having more friends,

I regret my dreams,

I am a selfish person who doesn't even deserve to be friends with Asa and Ayama.

I should go to school tomorrow,

No, people will judge me.

They will say "Owari, you haven't been to school in months! I thought you had died."

I don't want the attention.

I should tell someone.

No, I can't.

It's late and I'll just be bothering them.

Would people even care if I died?

No one at school would know the difference, and Asa and Ayama can do just fine without me.

It's too much pressure on me,

It's too much pressure on me,

It's too much pressure on me.

…

…

I want to rest but resting will only make me meet the figure again.

That distorted, contorted, devilish figure.

What is going on? Someone, please help me.

I clutched my chest and tears streamed down my face.

If I go now, no one can push me down. No one can get in my way when I'm gone.

The thought made me happy and put my mind to ease. I went back down.

Chapter 1B

Chapter 1B:
The Onlooker

I found myself wearing my uniform and heading off to school. I walked past the bridge faster than normal to not give in to that anymore. From now on, I will make it my mission to go to school! Even though there are only four days left…

     School started at 7:30 but I left at 6:00. I woke up at 5:50 because if I thought if I left early I'd have no time to second guess my decision. I also want to get there early to avoid running into people on the way there; it's simpler that way. After walking for a while, I got to the school and went into the main hall. I turned left from the main entrance, aimlessly moving in a random direction. Walking for a couple seconds made me realize I had forgotten which class I was in. There's a directory that shows which students are supposed to be in what classroom in the entrance area, so I went back and scoured the large sheet to find my name in the sea of other students. Sano, Owari…Class 3-4

Pictures, moments in time, sporting events, accolades, all things I had missed. I felt sentimental and reminiscent of times that I hadn't ever experienced before. As I walked the hallways, the silence was deafening. There was no outside sound; the school was almost like a black hole. My shoes off-puttingly echoed on the reflective wooden floors. The growing dissonance of my surroundings made me think back to a time when I was excited to go to school. Excited to be around people, make new friends, have new experiences, and most of all, be me. Somewhere in the last couple of years, this excitement and curiosity of the world vanished.

I got to the classroom and half expected everyone to be there. To my surprise, I opened the door and the teacher said, "Owari! Get to your seat! You know you're late, right?"

Everyone laughed, and I did too. I walked into the only empty seat, which was two rows from the back of the class and took out my notebook to start writing. We were learning about soil fertility today. I didn't think I was interested in soil fertility, but I'm excited, ready to learn, and will take everything in. I feel invigorated…like I was missing something this whole time and all I needed to do was turn on the ignition. Everyone was whispering behind the teacher's back as she was writing on the board, students were passing notes; the inaudible sounds of the classroom made me feel oddly comfortable. Someone was tapping their shoe, someone was whistling the tune to the big new radio hit, people were talking, people were unzipping their bags and taking out paper… I thought I strictly enjoyed the sounds of nature, but this doesn't seem so bad.

But as we know, none of this was the case. I walked in and sat in my seat two rows from the back. Putting my bag on my desk, I rested my head on it and closed my eyes.

Ten minutes passed, and I heard something opening. There was a couple of seconds pause, then a shut noise that was way louder than the first. It's almost as if they didn't mean to open whatever they did in the first place.

The opening noise happened once again. However, it was a very short note this time. At this point, I realized what had happened. Someone most likely opened the door, didn't expect me to be in here, got scared and closed it, then opened it back up slightly to watch me. I was pretending to be asleep now, and I had no intention of 'waking up' unless the person, whoever it was, talked to me first. About three more minutes passed and the room was still silent. Now that I was aware someone was there and was generally more alert, I would have heard them if they were to walk away, so they probably stayed by the door. I also stayed in my position.

Finally, I heard the door open a little more and footsteps were coming my way. They stopped at the front of my desk, and at this point, my heart was beating extremely fast. I wasn't sure if this person was some kind of creep intruder who was just going to stare at me all day or if it was another student. After an excruciatingly long couple of seconds, they tapped me on my shoulder… so I opened my eyes to look at them. …Miya! She looked so surprised, like she was unsure if it was actually me or not. I was surprised too. After all, I didn't expect anyone, especially Miya, to be here so early!

○

Miya is a quiet girl. She doesn't talk much to people she doesn't know, but once she becomes closer with you she can talk to you about almost anything to great lengths. If Ayama was academically intelligent, Miya was emotionally intelligent. Not to say Ayama wasn't emotionally intelligent or that Miya wasn't academically intelligent, but everyone has their strengths. Like I said before, she's pretty cold to people she's not familiar with, and she doesn't do well in populated spaces. I think that she feels a lot of pressure from a few select things, which is why she is the way that she is, but I won't get into that right now. Either way, I hope she can get over her anxiety one day and blossom into the fully realized version of herself that I know she can achieve, but I'd be lying if I said I didn't enjoy her standoffish attitude. She's the pure type, one who I could never see do any hard drugs or break any laws just for the thrill of it…but maybe that's just another thing she puts up around others. I don't like to speculate about things like that as much as one would assume; it makes me upset.

I don't think that Miya and Ayama like each other. This may be me being egocentric, but I feel as if they fight for my attention in a lot of ways. I think they feel as though they share a lot of personality traits on the surface, so I *have* to be friends with one or the other. Like, they think they fill the same role in my inner circle. I think that the only thing they share is that they're quiet around unfamiliar people, but Ayama rarely breaks out of her shell as opposed to Miya who does it frequently around me. Though, I suppose, Ayama will have never seen that side of her. Maybe one day Ayama and Miya can get to know each other better.

As we all know, too, of course, Asa is a very outgoing person, but even he gets shy around Miya sometimes. He's the type of guy who feels as though he needs to put on a performance of masculinity to appeal to the people he finds attractive, but stuff like that hasn't worked since the 1920s. This performance isn't himself, so he becomes awkward and self-conscious when he's around her. Because of this, he also slightly avoids her.

I think that the reason I haven't seen Miya in a while is that I often give in to the peer pressure of being around two people rather than one. It's easier to let down one person rather than two in most cases, however bad or wrong of me that may sound. Either way, I'd also be lying if I said that I didn't also feel this shyness around her. To me, she's one of the most beautiful people I've met... To be honest, I might've been interested in dating her if I knew what her plans after high school were. I say this because I don't think it'd be worth the heartache to become close for however long just to be separated again when she moves away. I've never actually asked her if she had any plans after high school, but only because I'd be afraid of getting asked that back.

○

"Owari..?"

"Miya! It's nice to see you."

"What are you doing here?"

"Well, I figured that since all the exams were over, and this would be one of my last chances to connect with our classmates, I'd come to school this final week. Plus we haven't spoken in a while, so I wanted to see you too." This wasn't necessarily true, because when I got up this morning I wasn't thinking about Miya. But it wasn't necessarily a lie either, I *was* genuinely happy to see her.

"Oh...and why are you here so early?"

"I was just about to ask you the same thing."

"Aha, it sounds like I'm interrogating you, let me sit down." She sat down in the seat to the left of me by the window. The beautiful sunrise reflected on her sparkling skin and her eyes glistened a shiny black.

Everything she did was so... elegant. I'm quite lucky for her to have been the one to come before anyone else.

"Well..." she said, pulling her long black hair behind her ear, "I actually get here in the morning before everyone else because I like the atmosphere of an empty school. It's kind of exciting being somewhere in a state you're not supposed to see it in. It's sort of like an amusement park that's vacant, or in the supermarket where the only sounds you can hear are the refrigerator buzzes; it's oddly comforting. I don't particularly enjoy doing my homework at home either, so I tend to do it before class starts."

I looked at my phone to see the time. "Oh, it's a quarter to seven, you don't have that much time left to do it."

"It's the final week, so the homework load isn't too much. We were just assigned to do a one-page paper on a reflection of our school life." She pulled out her laptop and opened up to a page where about half of it was filled with words. Looks like she was about halfway done.

Despite being a rural area, the school representatives decided this year to experiment and make the school a little more modern by letting students complete their work on laptops. I suppose they decided to experiment with us since it's such a small school; if it went awry it wouldn't matter too much. Although, I'm guessing it went well seeing as how Miya is still using her's.

"I really enjoy writing as you know...and I reflect on things in my life through my writing often, so this assignment is actually fun to me."

"Do you want to pursue writing?"

"It's my dream," she said, spinning a sparkly pink key chain through her fingers. "But I don't want to have to go to college for it. I don't need a professor to tell me how to write. I want to write according to my abilities; no one can tell me whether my writing is good or bad except me. Well...and a book publishing company I guess. But! A really big goal of mine is to start my own publishing company one day; I think it'd be fun. Not only would I be able to write for a living, but I'd also be able to read for a living. Could you just imagine me being a big CEO and having the privilege to cosign young aspiring writers and push their amazing work onto a bigger platform?" She had a warm smile on her face and crossed her arms vertically on her chest.

"I don't think something like that is too far off for you to be honest. I know that's what everyone would say in my position, but if I didn't believe in your abilities, I probably would have said something like, 'It's great to have big dreams', but I do honestly think you can do it."

"Really?? I hope I can too. My style of writing is very...surreal, I feel like? I don't try to make things confusing for the reader, but it always ends up becoming confusing. I think the most beautiful writing plays out like a dream sequence. I say this because trends are showing that this type of writing is becoming popular these days, especially with younger readers, which is my target demographic..." she said, trailing off her speech while turning her head from me to the window.

"Do you dream a lot, Miya?"

She turned back to me while staying captivated in the conversation like she never turned to begin with. "There are periods where I'll dream every day for a while, and then there are periods where I don't dream for months at a time. I don't think there's any set reason why that's the case... I don't think it's my mood or anything that affects whether I dream or not, I mean, well, whether I remember my dreams or not I guess. Anyways, my dreams usua- Oh, sorry, uhm- did you mean daydreaming? Like...do I dream about becoming a writer often?"

I smiled. "Either is okay, I'm interested in both."

She looked relieved and looked back out the window for a moment. "I have so many things on my mind constantly, it's hard to know what to say sometimes." She turned back to me and smiled. "That's probably why I like writing so much, I can write away all the things that I never get to say to people..."

We talked a little more about what exactly the contents of her essay were going to be, and I read some of the novels she had been working on for the past few months. Even though surrealism can usually be dissected into very logical thoughts and can reflect a person's mind, I didn't try analyzing her works and took it all at face value. Not because I didn't want to analyze, but because I was so excited to see her after months of not seeing her that it was distracting. As I would read, she would guide me through the confusing parts and describe what she was trying to convey. Some of the stuff she was describing I would've gotten without her help, but some of the stuff I was completely lost on. After she explained it though, I reread it and it made perfect sense. Thirty minutes flew by like nothing, and we were talking the whole time. It was refreshing talking to someone who wasn't Asa or Ayama.

The first bell rang and students hadn't arrived yet, but we could hear teachers arriving in our neighboring classrooms. I wish I had come to school every day to meet with Miya like this… but this magical effect surely wouldn't be as strong if I did.

"Do you want to…go somewhere with me after school, Miya?"

Miya started blushing but didn't hesitate to say yes.

I can tell how she's feeling by changes in her demeanor a lot of the time. When she's happy or excited, she tends to use a lot more ethereal-sounding words and her vocal inflections completely change. Hearing her excited tone of voice while saying yes made me happy.

Our teacher walked in shortly after the first bell but didn't say anything to me despite not seeing me in months. Not only did she not say anything, but she also didn't try to look surprised either. I'm sure she was surprised though. Slowly, other students walked in, and Miya walked back to her seat in her usual elegant and methodical manner in the front of the class by the door. Each student said the typical thing you'd expect when seeing me: "Hey! Owari! It's nice to see you. I hope you're doing well." …It was nice at first, but the effect quickly wore off.

Ayama eventually walked in, and we talked a little about my long-awaited return to the school. She was really happy that I had decided to come today. Asa also walked in, but only twenty minutes after class had officially started. The typical student after being late would usually quickly sit down and pick up where the class was to not fall behind, but not Asa. He saw me, ran over to his desk which is behind mine, and almost immediately asked me what felt like one hundred questions. It wasn't questions like Miya or Ayama had asked me, it was typical Asa questions.

Hours had gone by, and I had remembered why I don't go to school. The teacher would go on and on about topics that rarely interested me and no one was engaged. I remember everyone being somewhat engaged at the start of the year, but since we're all seniors in our last week, no one has the energy.

Everyone was silent minus the occasional Asa comment. This was not the bustling atmosphere I had imagined earlier in the day.

I phased in and out of listening to the teacher, but when I listened in for a moment she was going on about how the volcano south of Lake Tōya was due for an eruption soon. This interested me, so I listened in for the rest of the class.

The final bell rang, and it was off to the bridge we went. I packed up my things and went over to Asa and Ayama to head out of the class, relieved that the day was over. As I walked out of the main entrance, talking with Asa and Ayama about how my first day back was, I suddenly remembered... I asked Miya if she wanted to hang out this morning. Knowing Miya, I thought that she would purposefully take a while to leave the school to not be in the midst of the chaos that is the end of the school day, so I still had a chance to meet back up with her.

"I forgot something in the class! Don't wait for me, just head home guys!" I yelled as I started to run back into the school, almost tripping myself in the process.

"Heyy! Owari, where are you going? I can't walk home alone with Ayama!"

I didn't turn back to respond to him. I'm so dumb for forgetting.

I rushed back through the echoing empty halls once more and met Miya finally leaving the classroom. As I saw her in the doorway, I stopped running and put my hands on my knees. I was breathing heavily, and I could tell she was startled by me coming back.

"Owari...were you running?"

"I had forgotten that I asked you to hang out today! I came back as quickly as I could to make sure I could catch you leaving so we could go somewhere after."

"Oh..! That's very thoughtful of you. I sort of did feel awkward after you left with those two, but I didn't say anything because I thought our plans may have changed. They were on such short notice after all." As she said this, she turned her head to the side and looked disappointed. I don't think she was disappointed in me, just disappointed the whole situation happened in general. It's like she was disappointed at the fact she had gotten used to being let down so much in the past.

"I talk with Asa and Ayama every day. You're way more important right now."

She started walking past me. "Thanks. I appreciate you

saying that Owari. But it's okay, I need to finish this essay today! I need to continue to write before I get writer's block and can't do it anymore." She was now in the middle of the hallway walking towards the stairwell that led to the main entrance. She turned back to me just before descending the staircase, just as I had caught my breath and settled down. "Let's do it tomorrow, 'kay?"

I nodded without saying anything.

○

I arrived at the school at my normal time. Having had a pretty rough night, what I needed was to sit in a quiet room for a while and just take a breather. The weather was nice outside. The thing I like most about nature is the picturesque atmosphere it creates. It seems like time moves slower while moving in nature…like everything is exactly where it needs to be, so there's no need for change. I could feel the refreshing breeze brush past my legs and the smell of spruce filled the air.

I entered the main hall and started walking to my class. The reflection of my person on the floor glistened a blurry image, yet I felt very connected to my surroundings. My shadow kept me grounded. If it wasn't there, I would all but float away. I looked outside the window as I was walking down the hall, and the sky was painted a beautiful amber color. I stopped, turned to the window, held my arms out, and put them in a rectangular shape by forming two corners with my index and thumb fingers.

"Ka-chick."

I made it to my classroom and started to preemptively open my bag in preparation to take my laptop out while opening the door, but I was stopped by something. There was someone already in there. Someone was sleeping in one of the students' chairs! I quickly shut the door and my back impacted the wall outside. I slowly slid down the wall and held my knees up as I wrapped my arms around them. I started to breathe heavily. After a moment of trying to calm myself down, I realized that it was probably a homeless person who probably just needed to stay the night somewhere that was safe. I don't want to speculate how they got into school at night, but there was no time for that. Right now I needed to call security and get them escorted out immediately so I could resume my daily activities.

...

Ten minutes passed and I did nothing. I was too afraid to call someone. What if it wasn't an intruder and I'd be charged with disrupting the peace or something? Like, wouldn't I go to jail for that? Maybe I was just imagining things. After all, I didn't have the best of mornings, so it was definitely just a figment of my imagination.

I opened the door again slightly and peered through it. This person was carrying a bag. A bag…and…a school uniform! This was a classmate of mine! But…I didn't recognize them. Judging by what they're wearing, they had to be a guy …so…umm. …That did not narrow it down.

I quickly snapped back into reality. I felt even more anxious knowing that I was about to call security on a boy who wasn't doing anything wrong!

No, wait. No one ever comes this early. This is definitely a squatter who has dressed up in student's clothing as a way to trick the staff into letting him stay!

Stop! You're not making sense right now. Just open the door and walk up to him. It'll be okay.

I fully opened the door and swiftly made my way to

the desk so as to not have time to regret my decisions. I was mere inches away from him at this point, but his head was facing down and I couldn't tell by his hair alone who he was. All I know is, this "homeless person" was a male student who looked to be about 5'10 with medium-length black hair. I sighed and reluctantly tapped him on his shoulder. To get to eye level, I half bent down and pulled my hair behind my ear. Apparently, he was sleeping. He did the typical, 'Huh? I fell asleep?' routine that most of us do when we fall asleep in places that we're not used to, so it was good to know he was at least human.

After his initial daze, he opened his eyes and turned his head to me. When he saw me, he pushed his chair back slightly and had to be fully awake at this point.

"Owari…?"

"Miya! It's nice to see you!"

To my surprise, the man I once proclaimed was a squatter… was just my friend, Owari. We bonded in our second year a lot and texted sometimes too. We were very close friends, and over the time I've known him, he's helped me grow a lot as a person. This came to an end however when he stopped attending school. Nothing happened between us, but it was a mutual falling out of sorts.

One day, he randomly just didn't go to school. I wasn't worried, people miss school once or twice all the time. Soon, this 'one day' turned into a week. I was starting to get worried. We were close at the time, so I thought that if I was 'important' to him, he would text me and tell me what was going on or just come to school and explain it to me in person. I never received a text, and I never spoke to him again after that. At first, I had waited a month. My thought process was, "Maybe he has some type of family issue or is sick, so a couple of weeks may be too little time to recover. I'll give it a month, and if I don't hear back, I'll text him asking if he's okay." A month passed, and I was too nervous to text him. I woke up one day on a weekend and said to myself, "Okay Miya! After breakfast, you'll text him, 'Are you okay? I miss you.'" Breakfast came and went. "Okay Miya! After you shower, you'll text him, 'Are you okay? I'm getting worried.'" I showered. "Okay Miya! Write for a couple of hours, and when you get tired, you'll text him, 'Please be okay. I'm worried sick.'"

I wrote and didn't stop writing until 2:00 am. I was avoiding messaging him at all costs out of embarrassment that

I was overreacting about him being out.

My wrists were sore, and I was breaking down in tears. "I can't text him anymore, it's 2:00 am. If I were to get a message asking if *I* was okay at 2:00 am, I wouldn't know what to think."

This cycle of preparing myself to message him but always failing to do so went on for the rest of the week, but I quickly forgot about it as the new week started. Forgot may not be the right word...I just chose to block the whole situation from my head. The week went on though, and I thought about him every day. I would still sometimes think, "After school ends, I'll message him." I never did of course, but the good thing about it was that when I didn't end up doing it, I wouldn't as feel guilty as I did last week.

And so, the week came and went, and then the month, and then a few months… and I slowly thought about him less. When I did occasionally think about him, it was for a split second, and the thought of messaging him to ask if he was okay never appeared alongside.

I had freed myself from this anxiety, but at what cost? I lost a friend because I was too anxious to say 'Hi'? Why am I like this…? This is so unfair to me…and Owari. What if he was waiting for me to message him or show up at his door one day and hug him and say that I missed him. What if we were at a standstill and thinking the exact same thing right now. What if he was also up at 2:00 am wanting to message me telling me he's okay, telling me he'll come back soon…but was too anxious to do it…

Wait, but this isn't all on me, right? Owari is equally as responsible for our falling out. Friendship is a two-way street. Unless one of you does something egregiously wrong without being provoked, both parties are to blame one hundred percent of the time, right?

Even though I had forgotten about him for a couple of months, these sudden intrusive thoughts plagued my mind with guilt every second of the day. My only escape was to write, but even when I wrote, I realized I would write about him. My only other escape was to sleep, but it was hard to. It's crazy to me how one random thought can change the trajectory of months of your life. Looking at it logically, nothing had changed in the leading months to having this initial thought, and after having the thought, nothing had changed between us then too. So if nothing had changed, and I was once perfectly content with not feeling guilty about not talking to him, then I shouldn't feel guilty now, right?

...I found myself not going to school one day too.

"If Owari can do it...then I can too..." I told myself.

One day turned into a week. Now it was Sunday night, and I had no plans of going to school the next day.

New Message from: *Ayama*
> → Hey Miya. I'm worried about you since you haven't been to school in a while. Are you okay?

This is just what I wanted. Someone to finally notice and care about me. The thought that I was simply an attention-seeking asshole crossed my mind briefly, but I was too excited to care. I responded almost immediately.

> I'm okay Ayama. Thank you so ←
> much for checking in on me.
> I appreciate it a lot. I've just
> been sick with something this
> week, but I'll be back to my
> normal self tomorrow.

→ I'm really glad to hear that. I can now sleep with my mind at ease :D. See you tomorrow.

See you then. ←

I was ecstatic at first. Ayama, of all people, was the person who messaged me. Not that I was close with anyone else at school, so I don't know who else I would have been expecting, but Ayama was somehow still a pleasant surprise.

I wallowed in the thought of getting a message from someone, but now that the conversation was over, I had an empty void in my chest. Was I too cold? I knew that after I said "See you then." the conversation was over, but if she *really* cared, wouldn't she have responded? Even if it was just like...a smiley face? Can't someone put in just a little effort when talking to me for once? If I was more animated, she probably would've conversated with me more.

No, no. The conversation ended. It's late. She said she was going to sleep. She's tired right now. She texted you even though she was tired. Please be grateful for that. Stop worrying.

I took three deep breaths and made my way to the shower. Even though it was late, and I was tired as well, I hadn't showered all week and I needed to be presentable for school tomorrow.

I quickly got undressed and stepped into the shower. I turned the water on slightly hot but progressively turned the heat up more and more as my skin got comfortable with it. As the water was running down my body…something changed. I felt as if I was being cleansed. Not just cleansed physically but cleansed of all the guilt that had swelled up inside me. I looked down, and the water was satisfyingly funneling down the drain. I visualized each thought as the flowing water, and as the water was being drained, each thought was escaping my mind in rapid succession.

I'm not good enough

Owari doesn't like me

Ayama doesn't like me

The world doesn't care about me

These thoughts all trickled into the drain like water.

For the first time in a while, I felt good about myself. I stepped out of the shower, dried myself, and looked in the foggy mirror. I walked closer to the mirror, leaned forward over the sink, and touched my forehead against the mirror. The fog around my eyes cleared up and it grounded me even more than I already was. I laughed to myself for a moment and wondered why I was so anxious in the first place. Maybe I'll try my hair differently tomorrow?

I didn't have a hard time sleeping that night.

○

I don't like saying this, and I'd hate for someone to feel like I'm bragging or am egocentric, but I've never been that self-conscious about my looks... at least when I'm alone. I know that I'm an attractive person. There are downsides of course, but there are downsides to every type of look someone has. I'm not one to negatively judge someone else's appearance, and each person has a different way of describing each other, so this all is just my arbitrary opinion to preface what I'm about to say.

When you're deemed "too skinny", I'd imagine the type of comments you'd get would be along the lines of, "Why don't you eat enough?"... When you're deemed "too overweight", I'd imagine the type of comments you'd get would inversely be, "Why do you eat so much?"... When you're "too tall", people will ask you to do things for them, and if you're "too short" people will patronize you like you're a little kid. The downside of my type is that people stare, but rarely will people say what they're thinking to my face, so it's okay. Well, logically, it's okay. But emotionally, I get stressed out a ton. I don't like places with a lot of people for this reason. I feel as though since I look the way I do, I'm supposed to act how everyone expects someone like me to act. In TV dramas, it'd be the popular girl who has an unlimited number of friends and will grow up to be a famous model on social media… But that's not me at all, and people don't expect that. And although it bothers me quite a bit…it's been getting better recently. I've been learning to overcome this fear of judgment from others, and when I get compliments from people I actually appreciate it rather than becoming more self-conscious about the thing they mentioned. If someone were to ask me how to get over this anxiety, I'd have to say…I don't know. I'm not exactly sure how I got over it in the first place. Well, Owari helped me a lot, to be honest. He's been one of the few people who've treated me normally in high school. The thing he told me is that most people when they're staring, kind of…completely forget about it when they stop. So, although they might be thinking whatever for the fifteen seconds they're staring, it'll eventually go away like it never happened at all when they stop. Another thing I realized is that this anxiety wasn't directly because of my appearance, just the expectations people put on me because of it. Realizing and thinking through both of these things made me feel so much better. So scratch what I said before; if someone were to open up to me about feeling similarly, I'd know exactly what advice to give them. No one has really opened up to me, but I think I'd comfort people by telling them what I'd want to hear if I were them. Everyone's different and everyone will react to things differently, so I'm sure it wouldn't always work out, but most of the time I'm confident it'd turn out great in the end.

One would assume that thinking about things that have made me anxious in the past would be something I wouldn't want to do, but in this case, I mainly do it to remind myself I have the power to overcome it all, which is why I brought it up in the first place. It's refreshing to think about the positive times I've had with Owari rather than focusing on the negative times and feeling guilty about them. He's helped me so much, so wherever he is right now, I'm sure he's doing well. But I can't owe it all to him, I've helped myself out a lot too.

○

"What are you doing here?"

I sat down and looked forward to catching up with him. We talked for a little and I told him about my dream of being a writer. He knew about it before today, but I think he just viewed my passion for writing as a hobby rather than something I'd like to pursue in the future. At the end of our conversation, he asked me if I wanted to go with him someplace after school. Of course, I replied yes. I wouldn't love anything more than to do that, especially after being away from each other for so long.

Students arrived one after another, and I went back to my normal seat in the front as class started. I was paying attention to the teacher for the most part, but I was mainly just thinking about what Owari and I could do later…We could go to the park, we could write together, we could bring a speaker to the lake and play music, we could do all sorts of things. My mind raced and I got butterflies in my stomach.

School flew by and I was packing my things when I saw Owari, Ayama, and Asa walk out of the class without me. Maybe he's just seeing them off to the door and then coming back?

I waited in the class for a while, but it took him longer than I would've thought to walk to the door and back, so I assumed he forgot about me. I was dumb to think that he was going to come back. I mean, I didn't message him once over the half a year he was gone, so I guess it makes sense. I thought we had bonded this morning and patched things up between us, but I guess it was just a fluke. I am so done with thi-

Breathe. It's okay. If he comes tomorrow, you can talk to him about what is happening right now and I'm sure it'll be just one big misunderstanding. If you have to pick a time to worry, worry if he doesn't show up tomorrow. Now that you know he's well, too, you can message him freely without worrying you'll bother him. You were worry-free for two months, and seeing Owari is what you've been wanting for those two months, so try not to mess up this moment.

After my thirty-second breather, I stood up and made my way to the door. ...There he was, standing by the door in a pose that someone would make if they were out of breath and just stopped running.

He had actually come back. I was elated, of course, and once he explained to me what happened, I didn't mind as much as I thought I would have. He seemed genuinely sorry for leaving without me, but I told him that we could hang out tomorrow because I had to do schoolwork tonight. The truth was, I had already finished my assignment throughout the day, so I had no more work to do. The reason I said what I did was because I wanted to give him more incentive to show up tomorrow. I wanted to spread this period of bliss through at *least* a few days and not explode from happiness in just one day.

Today was good, I enjoyed it more than I thought I ever thought I would have. And it's all thanks to one person.

○

As I saw her walk away, I was relieved. She didn't look mad or disappointed as I originally thought. She looked content.

I went out of the school through the back entrance since it was shorter to get to the bridge that way and because I needed to catch up to Asa and Ayama before they got too far. I started a speed walk of sorts, but since I was in a good mood, I went through an alternative path by going through the river rather than going around it. It's not really a path, it's more like a set of big rocks that are planted on the river, but I'll call it a path anyways.

I was jumping from rock to rock on the river and I felt like an astronaut. I imagined myself in slow motion... jumping and jumping. Imagining myself going slowly actually helped me keep my balance. I think if I imagined myself as a ninja or samurai that had to traverse a dangerous path extremely quickly to escape some sort of assailant, I would have fallen.

I reached the steep riverbed on the opposite side of where I came from and hoisted myself onto the same elevation as the main path. At this point, I was fairly certain they were still pretty far ahead, so I needed to take a shortcut to catch up. I continued down the path and saw a young man in his early twenties in front of me about one hundred feet away. As I got closer, I recognized him...he makes up half of the couple that I see on the bridge every day at 4:00 pm. As we walked past each other, I made sure not to make eye contact. Not because I was embarrassed, but because I assumed he probably wasn't in the best of moods, so it was just out of courtesy.

The shortcut I was cutting through eventually leads back to the main path I usually walk on, but not after going through the cliff area. This area is a shortcut because there are a lot of cliffs and mountains, and instead of going around the mountain, you can go directly through it. I haven't been near one of the cliff's edges recently, but I'd estimate around a one-hundred-foot fall if you were to somehow slip off. We don't usually take this path because, even though it's technically a shorter distance to our homes, it's just too inconvenient most days I guess.

I had gotten off the flat path and veered left at a crossroads to get to the incline; leading me up to the top of the mountain where I'd just go right back down. At the summit, there's a clearing that's mostly used for recreation. Even though it can be seen as pretty dangerous to recreationally be around somewhere like that, people simply stay away from the edge and do whatever they want to away from any harm. Right after the cliffs, more specifically on the other side of this mountain, is where I usually walk home. Even though it's a pretty steep incline on this side, the mountain modestly lowers in elevation on the other side. While walking up the incline, a frantic-looking woman rushed past me. It was the same woman I had seen running yesterday as well. I didn't want to think of what she could have been doing this whole time, but it seemed as though she was looking for something. We walked past each other, not saying a word. However, soon after I thought I was in the clear, she called out to me.

"Excuse me, sir!"

I turned around. I had to look down at her since she was lower on the incline, and we were pretty far away at this point to be talking at a normal level, so she started to move closer to me. As she was walking, the wind started to pick up. I could tell she was struggling moving up the incline, and her face was scrunched out of what looked like deep concern. One hand was holding up her dress from getting dirty on the path, and the other hand was holding one of those new-age floppy straw hats from flying away in the wind. She walked up closer to me and was about three feet away from me at this point.

"Yes?"

"I've been looking for my son…have you seen anyone age ten wandering near here today?"

"No I haven't, but if you give me a description of him, I'll be on the lookout and if I find him I'll report to the police."

"The police?"

"Yes, the police. Have you not filed a missing person's report yet?" I asked this because I knew that her son had been missing *at least* since last night.

"No...I haven't thought about that. I've been so stressed out that I haven't had the time to do that. Plus, at first, I didn't think it was that serious, so that wasn't on my mind. And...don't you have to wait forty-eight hours to do that?"

"That's a common myth, you can report it the second they go missing and police will be on the lookout. I don't mean to worry you even more, but the longer you wait, the less likely it is that someone will find them." I paused for a moment, thinking if what I said was appropriate given the situation. "Anyways," I continued, "you needn't worry about having to do this a second time."

"What is that supposed to mean?"

I could see how that would mean that she would never find her son again, but what I was implying was that, after she found him, he'd see how worried she was and be more careful in the future. I explained this to her, but it seemed as though she didn't buy it. To be honest, I probably wouldn't have believed myself either if I were her, but I can't take back my poor choice of words now, so I have to roll with it.

"Where did you last see him?"

"Three days ago..."

She went on to explain he was going to play with his friend at the park. After they went to the park, they were going to go to the town center to get some food and then head home. To be quite honest, I'm shocked that she would let her ten-year-old son go with a friend to all those places alone, but, if she had the choice, I'm sure she would take it all back... so I can't fault her for that now. She told me a little more about him. She described his physical appearance, what he was wearing, and what his voice sounded like. I asked if she had talked to his friend's parents about the situation, but she didn't even know *who* the friend was, much less the parents, so that was a no-go.

I got her to stop worrying eventually, told her to call the police and file a missing person report and go home to rest. I can't imagine she got much sleep knowing that her ten-year-old son was out somewhere all alone. The woman left down the incline and pulled out her phone. I turned back around and headed towards the summit once more.

On the right side of me, there were lines of spruce and pine trees that produced a certain aroma that I can't describe. Mixed with the crisp spring weather, it had all the perfect conditions for a picnic. That's actually what most families do at the summit, they have picnics, but I hadn't had one before. I stopped and enjoyed the scenery for a couple of minutes, then remembered that I should probably tell Ayama and Asa what happened. After remembering, I was pretty on edge. At this point, I had been talking to her for a good ten minutes, so I felt bad for Asa and Ayama. I didn't know if they were waiting for me somewhere or if they had just left me to go home alone. When planning things, I usually text Ayama over Asa. I don't trust him enough to respond, much less have his phone on him. I opened up our chat and started typing, asking where they were, when suddenly I heard someone crying. At first, I thought that it must have been the woman. When she pulled out her phone, I imagine she called the police to file a report, so maybe they told her some bad news. I turned around, ready to run back down and ask what happened, but when I turned around, no one was there. The crisp, atmospheric spring weather quickly turned into an eerie and unsettling coldness. I no longer felt safe in my surroundings and being alone didn't make that any better. I put away my phone at this point and listened in. The cries were coming from above me! Someone must be at the top of the mountain. What if the boy was looking for his mother and he couldn't find *her*? I ran up to the mountain as fast as I could but saw no one. The sudden chills I had gotten while I first heard the cries faded away by now, but I was still very much on edge. Someone was still crying, so I listened closely to find exactly who or what the noise was coming from. As I listened, I moved; it was almost instinctual.

I had scoured the perimeter of the clearing, but I still found no one. At this point I was grasping at straws, but I went on one more lap around the edges of the cliffs to see if I could find anyone. As I reached a particular edge, the crying was louder than it ever was. I still couldn't see anyone, so I had no choice but to assume that whatever was crying was under me. I cautiously looked over the cliff's edge, the cliff that, if you were to fall, you'd be falling for over one hundred feet, and there he was...the woman's son.

He was hanging from a tree branch off the cliff. He was about three feet below me, so if I reached my arm down, I could surely grab him. As I looked, he was looking down at the valley that he would have faced if I hadn't been there to help him. I yelled, "Hey!" But he didn't look up. He was so panicked that he had most likely shut out all outside stimulus and was just focusing on using all his strength to hang on to the branch. Coincidentally, as I yelled to him though, another finger slipped off the branch. His hands were red and bruised, so he had been here for a long time. A couple of hours at least.

"Hey!" I yelled louder this time hoping he would hear me.

He acknowledged me by turning his head up to look. His eyes were red and the veins in his neck were unnaturally bulging. He continued crying as if the situation hadn't changed, which wasn't surprising to me, but now that he knew I was here, I knew I could help him.

"Hey. I'm going to help you, okay? I'm a friend of your mother's. Grab my arm and I'll hoist you up to safety."

"Y-You know, *krgn*, m-my mom?"

"Of course. The one with the big floppy straw hat, right?"

He started smiling. He now knew that we were talking about the same people and trusted me.

"I know it's hard, but try and use your other hand to grab my arm."

"I-I can't feel it. I lost circulation a l-long time ago."

"Okay. Start shaking it and put your full concentration into waking it up. Here, I'll even help, 'Excuse me Lefty, please wake so we can bring you to safety!'"

He started moving his arm a little.

"Did that help?"

"Mh-mm. He's awake now."

I reached out my arm and he grabbed it. The battle wasn't over yet, but I could tell he felt much safer and calmer than he had before. I wasn't sure if I had the strength to pull up a ten-year-old by myself, but I had to be confident. Having always heard stories about mothers who can lift cars to save their child's life purely through adrenaline, I knew something like this wasn't impossible.

I was pulling him up inch by inch when my phone suddenly vibrated in my pocket. This set me off guard more than it should have. While pulling him up, I twisted my body to the side and my phone fell out. I quickly glanced over at the screen and read the message that had made it vibrate moments before.

1 min Old Message from: *Ayama*
 → 'Wari. Where are u?? We've been waiting @ the usual spot for a while lol .

She must have been talking about the bridge. But I couldn't right now. I can't respond. Saving this child's life is much more important than Ayama worrying about where I am. I can't believe I even took a millisecond to consider anything other than saving him just now. I was straining so much to pick him up that I was starting to lose strength. We had been making steady progress as I had been trying this for about two minutes now. He was probably about a foot away from being able to get enough strength to grab the ledge himself.

Straining. Straining. Stray- My vision went black. I was still conscious, but I imagine a lack of blood in my brain blurred my vision.

I've known Ayama and Asa for six years, right? Since…yeah. Six years. Shouldn't I care way more about them in this situation than this kid? I mean, they've probably been waiting by the bridge for about twenty minutes now without knowing if I would come back or not. They must be worried sick; I have to go to them. Please, someone, give me the strength to get me out of this situation as soon as possible.

Suddenly, I got the strength, but not the kind I originally wanted. I was panting heavily; I had been holding my chest so tightly from the stress that I wasn't getting enough oxygen to my lungs. I...I don't know this kid or his mother. This might not even *be* the kid that went missing. Where is his friend? Where...

He does look like what she described, but his clothes are so muddy that I can't tell if it matches. I...I'm...probably never going to see his mother again. Therefore, I shouldn't care what happens to her, or the consequences if I let him go. Wait, what? What consequences? No one would know I *willingly* let go even though I could have picked him up. ...But we were so close now, maybe about five inches away from safety.

All at once, I stopped straining. Asa and Ayama were waiting for me. I'm with them almost every day. The consequences of making those two upset, as opposed to the consequences of this child's mother being upset, are not on the same level. Plus, if I let this kid go, I'll never have to see him again. This was perfect. My mask was finally coming off. This is me revealing my true colors. This is the real me, the me that doesn't care about what others think. I was wrong, I'm not doing this for Asa or Ayama, I'm doing this...for me.

The tightness in my chest loosened, and I could finally rest by laying on the ground with my legs dangling off the edge.

As I lay there, I closed my eyes and I heard it. It was a loud continuous noise that went on for around three seconds before it suddenly stopped.

○

Why would I have to pretend I like someone? If I don't like someone, I don't interact with them, and if I don't interact with them, they'll have no impact on my life. How is it logical to pretend to like someone with no impact on my life? If I'm only going to see someone once, such as a random passerby, there'd be no reason to not scream randomly around them; if I don't interact with them again, they'll have no impact on my life. Why would I care about what someone thinks if that person has no impact on my life? Now, is it normal to randomly scream? No. But doing it solely because you have the ability to, gives you the freedom and confidence to do things that are actually productive in the future. If I scream now, I can do all sorts of things later. Picking up that next-to-worthless coin on the ground may mean nothing now, but picking up every next-to-worthless coin you see in the next ten years will lead you to grow an empire of next-to-worthless coins that seemingly out of nowhere became coins that are the opposite of next-to-worthless. The idea that you don't need to be socially acceptable, especially around those who have no impact on your life is a great idea at first...But if everyone were to do it I guess it'd be out of hand. But everyone will never do it, which is actually why something like this is in the realm of possibility.

People will claim I am simply a nihilist or contrarian, but neither is true. It is simply impossible to be a nihilist. It is, by definition, a complete contradiction. I am not a contrarian simply for the fact that what I'm arguing is not opinion-based. The only reason I have to argue in the first place is because mentally willed people need to self-actualize and destroy all the barriers that restrained them from realizing this themselves.

Thinking about this more, no one can truly believe in every principle of a single philosophy, because any extreme is impossible for a person to meet. Although I believe that there isn't any higher power that controls our actions such as fate or destiny, being a realist does seem pretty bleak, even for me. I don't think limiting ourselves by using labels is necessary because our view of things is, in reality, a gray jumbled-up mess, but grouping ourselves into something and identifying with someone; anyone, can make us feel a little less alone.

◯

I heard footsteps running up to me but I kept my eyes closed.

"Owari!! Are you okay!?"

"Do I need to perform mouth to mouth?!"

Hm? It was Asa and Ayama? How did they know I was here? I opened up my eyes and turned my head almost to the point where half of my face was touching the ground and I looked up and back slightly. "I'm okay…how did you guys know I was up here?"

Ayama got closer and squatted down next to me. "We heard someone scream from up here so we got worried."

"Yeah."

"Weren't you two waiting at the bridge?"

"Oh, so you saw my text? Well…you didn't respond so we thought you might've got hurt somewhere so we started walking back to see if we could find you…"

"And find you we did! Why were you screaming?"

"Asa, it wasn't him screaming. Couldn't you tell by the voice?"

"Uhm…yeah I guess. I was just testing you, honestly."

"I believe it." She rolled her eyes playfully and smiled as Asa squatted down next to me as well. "So...are you okay Owari?"

"Yes, I'm okay."

"What was that screaming noise?"

"There were a couple of kids playing up here, but they went down the other side of the mountain... on the steep side."

"...And why are you laying down?"

I didn't know how to make an excuse for that. Should I just come clean and say what *actually* happened? I don't know if they would turn me in...but if anyone were to...I guess it'd be Ayama? I don't know.

"I...figured that you had already gone home and left by now, so I thought I'd admire the scenery while I can and stay here for a while."

"That's okay, but you have to respond to people when they message you, or else they'll get worried."

"I know, but it being my first day back and everything I was really tired and didn't have the energy to respond back."

My phone buzzed again, and I turned my head in the opposite direction to check it. It was Miya asking if I had gotten home okay. I read the message, turned off my phone, then went right back to my original position, eyes closed, looking at the sky.

"Who was that Owari? I thought you didn't have any other friends," Asa blurt out.

"Well, I do." I opened my eyes reluctantly.

"What?? At first, I was just making fun of how lonely you were, but now that I know it *was* a friend of yours…I'm completely offended!" Asa stood up and made a righteous pose while looking at the sky. "To be quite honest, I'm unsure why you would even need another friend beside me!"

"Asa, what about me?!," Ayama stood up and looked at Asa, frustrated.

"Oh." Asa's face completely froze. I didn't know for sure, but I was fairly certain that he had completely forgotten Ayama was there. He could've played it off better to make her less mad with him, but she was thinking the same thing I was.

"Ughh," she groaned.

Ayama started walking away without us, so I quickly stood up and started walking after her. She was walking at a slightly faster pace, so I had to start speed walking to catch up. When I did, I put my hand on her shoulder and asked if she was okay. She moved her shoulder to where my hand wasn't on it anymore, irritated.

She crossed her arms. "I've been trying so hard today. But Asa said that, and it was the last straw."

I didn't know if it was insensitive to think that Ayama was above this kind of childish fit.

"Trying hard? Did something happen?"

"We were trying so hard to look for you and I didn't even get a thank you. And then with everything Asa just said…it's too much."

Asa had caught up to us at this point but didn't say anything. Ayama dropped her arms and slightly drooped her head. She slowly turned around and I was surprised to see tears streaming down her face. She started moving toward me and held her arms out for a hug. I held mine out and hugged her before she whispered, "I'm…just tired. You didn't do anything wrong, okay? Don't feel bad."

I looked down at her. "I'm the one who should be comforting you, Ayama. Try not to worry too much."

"Kay…"

She let go and turned to Asa. She was embarrassed by the fact she got so upset in front of both of us, so when she turned to him, her face got red and she put her head down again. She put her hands together in front of her torso and apologized to Asa as well.

"It's like Owari said, we're the ones who are sorry."

"Yeah...I guess so. I uhm... think I want to head home alone today...but...I'll message you both when I get home so you know I got there safe."

"No worries, have a goodnight Ayama."

"See you tomorrow."

Ayama started walking off in the direction they had come from. We stood still till she was no longer in our vision.

"I'm going to head home alone too, Asa."

"Okay. But you don't have to text me when you get there."

"Wasn't planning on it," I replied facetiously.

"Whatever, I wasn't going to message you either."

I went back to the cliff's edge, grabbed my phone off the ground, then started heading in the direction Ayama had gone in. I noticed that Asa didn't move for as long as we were in each other's field of vision, so I hope he started walking back as well when he couldn't see me anymore.

I checked my phone to see the time and forgot that Miya had texted me. Even though something huge just happened, I felt bad that this is the second time I had forgotten about her today.

14 min Old Message from: *Miya☆*

→ Did you make it home okay?

Hey Miya. I stopped for a ←
little at the park to relax
but now that it's getting a
little darker I'm heading back.

I don't like texting as much as talking to someone in person, but for some reason, I elaborate on things over text more. She responded in under a minute.

→ I haven't been there in a
while, let's go together for a
picnic! I'll bring the supplies.
>:) .

After what just happened, I don't think I want to be back here for a while, but maybe tomorrow I'll shake it off and be okay again. The idea of a picnic really excites me.

I'll hold you to that! ←

I put my phone on silent and put it back in my pocket. Not because I didn't want to talk to Miya anymore, but because the conversation was over and I didn't want to unexpectedly feel a buzz and get startled again. Before I did this though, I put on my headphones and shuffled songs I like to help calm me down.

"...Mm mm mm mm mm mm, mm mm mm mm, hm mm mm mm, hmm mm mm mm hmm hmm hmm…"

I was walking back home..and I felt this paranoid feeling. A feeling so unsettling that I had to turn around and look behind me to make sure that no one was following me. No one was there, so I felt a little better for the time being.

"...Mm mm mm mm mm mm, mm mm mm mm, hm mm mm mm, hmm mm mm mm hmm hmm hmm…"

I turned back around to the direction I was walking and put my hands in my pockets.

"...Mm mm mm mm mm mm, mm mm mm mm, hm mm mm mm, hmm mm mm mm hmm hmm hmm…"

I laughed to myself a little bit, what could I have been so worried about? I once again started to admire the scenic walk I was on, but something stuck out to me. Multiple things stuck out to me. As I was walking past a field of flowers, all of the flowers had eyes. Huge, white eyes that were moving to look at me as I was walking.

> "...Mm mm mm mm mm mm, mm mm mm mm, hm mm mm mm,

I didn't know what was wrong with me. I closed my eyes for a second and looked back at the field... there were no eyes. I randomly thought to myself, 'No eyes, only I.' When I thought of that, I repeatedly said it in my head while the music was still playing

> "...Mm mm mm mm mm mm, mm mm mm mm, hmn mm hm..."

No eyes, only I. No eyes, only I. No eyes, only I. No eyes...

The streetlight was staring at me. Now, this was different. The eyes were no longer a couple of inches in diameter, the eye that was ogling me had to have been at least a foot in diameter. Even though it was fifteen feet above me, it was so big that I could see its veins. I stared at it for so long that I caught a glimpse of it blinking. When I kept walking, I thought that its blinking would have made it stop staring, but as soon as it opened its eye back up, it kept looking at me like this omnipotent being that never closed its eye in the first place.

"...Mm   mm

mm mm mmn..."

I was getting sick of the song that was playing. I took my headphones out and started running back home. The wind started picking up and the blades of grass were more horizontal than vertical. The trees were swaying and were making a loud 'SHHHHHHHHH' sound. All the sounds of any animals also stopped. The bugs stopped creaking and the birds stopped chirping. Usually, you'd see at least one person on the path, but I didn't see anyone as I was running. How did I simultaneously feel the most alone I'd ever felt while also feeling like the whole world was watching me? The setting sun was behind a mountain now, so I couldn't see the full thing, but the top half of it was also staring at me. Now an eye hundreds of thousands of miles long was staring at me like no tomorrow.

I picked up speed. As I was running, I clutched my bag and barely had my eyes open from the wind. Because of this, I tripped on a stray root that had persevered through the compacted dirt and now my knees and elbows were bloodied.

I had no time to stop though. I kept running. Tears welled up in my eyes from the combination of the wind, my new cuts, and the guilt of what I had done. I had disappointed everyone in the end, so my actions earlier meant nothing.

I reached my home and didn't take my shoes off at the door. I ran into the house, running over everything. The lamp at the table fell and made a loud crash; my bag had hit my dad's pill bottle on the counter and all the pills scattered on the floor. I didn't look back. I ran into my room and hid in my closet.

I sat down in the small, quiet, dark space with my knees up and my arms wrapped around them. I scrambled to to take out my phone, but since the closet was so small I hit my elbow on the wall while taking it out. I screamed in pain and threw my phone into the little space next to me out of frustration. I turned, kneeled down, and my position could have been compared to someone who was facing the imminent threat of a bomb. I clenched my fist and hit it repeatedly on the ground. Since I was on my knees, the cuts were getting even more irritated, and I was putting myself through more pain. I kept banging for a couple of minutes but eventually got tired and shut down. Once calm, I checked my phone like I was planning on doing before. It had a small crack on the side. I turned on the power button and the blue glow from the screen illuminated my face. I closed my eyes for a few seconds and opened them back up slowly so they could adjust to the sudden flash of light.

27 min Old Message from: *Ayama*
→ I'm home. Sorry for earlier.
I'll see you at school tomorrow.

I didn't have it in me to respond. I fell asleep in my closet that night.

Interlude 2

We were walking on the path. I was tired, so I was being carried by my dad.

"Dad, why don't we live in the city?" I asked him, eyes closed, laying my head down on his shoulders.

"We used to live in the city around six years ago, back when you were just born."

I felt myself slipping down, so he boosted me back up to where it was comfortable on his arms. "And why did we move?"

"Well, generally, it's a lot less safe in a big city. Plus, I grew up in the country, so it's more comfortable for me to stay here too," he said as he looked up at the bright blue sky through the overhanging branches.

"You seem like you don't like it all too much…"

"I don't, Owari. That's why we moved. Plus, I like to stay connected with nature as much as I can."

"Then why'd you move to the city in the first place?" I had a feeling he was leaving out some part of his story, so to intimidate him I brought my head off of his shoulder and straightened my back.

"We have a lot of relatives in the city, so it only made sense to move with them at the time. Your grandmother and grandfather separated when I was young, so I lived with grandma alone in the countryside while growing up. On the other hand, my other siblings and grandpa lived in the city."
He looked back at me and smiled, but I was very confused at this point. Not only for the reason he was smiling but for his whole story in general. He continued, "When you're young, it's easy to want to go to the city, explore, and try new things to see what sticks. But it just wasn't for me. Plus, if we keep it between us, our family name is kind of famous in Tokyo and I didn't like the attention.

"Famous? You mean I'm famous??" My eyes sparkled

and I was waving my legs back and forth.

The movement got uncomfortable for him, so he put me down and let me walk beside him. "Our last name is Sano, just like the big electronics company in Tokyo, Sano。 Corp. Didn't you ever make that connection?" he asked jokingly.

"There's a company with our last name?"

"Boy, you sure have lived in the country for too long. You don't even know about Sano。 ?"

I looked down at the dirt path with a frown. "No...I didn't know. I'm sorry."

"There's no reason to be sorry, there'd be no way of you knowing about it unless I told you, and I didn't tell you about them for this long for a reason."

"What? You didn't want me to know I'm famous?" I looked up at him again, my mouth slightly ajar in anticipation of his answer.

"The company doesn't have the best reputation in Tokyo, people kind of...look down on it, so I sort of hid it from you so you weren't embarrassed about your last name. And like I said, I don't really like the attention from people, so when people ask if we're related to the company's founder we always say "no", remember?"

"Now that you say it, people have come up to me asking if it's like the electronics company." I looked down again, worried.

"Keep your head up, 'Wari." He gently slapped my back to keep my eyes off the ground. "Don't be sad, I chose to tell you this now because I knew you're strong enough to not let that stuff bother you. It's important to know where you come from, don't be ashamed."

"But aren't you ashamed?"

"No, I'm not ashamed. You can not want to talk about things and still be comfortable with them, you know."

"...I didn't know that."

"You're strong enough to not let it bother you, right?"

…

"Yes. I'm strong enough."

Chapter

2A

Chapter 2A: Despondence

I was woken up by the sound of my alarm at 5:30 am and reluctantly turned it off after around fifteen beeps. While I was turning the alarm off on my phone, I checked my notifications. None. I don't know why I expect any, but each day I look it's disappointing for some reason. Sometimes I purposefully don't check my phone throughout the day so I don't get disappointed over and over again about the fact that there are no new messages from anyone. I'd rather just be disappointed once.

    Similar thoughts ran through my mind for the next ten

minutes while I lay in bed staring at the ceiling.

"This is okay, everything is okay. Today is going to go great." I whispered to myself as motivation to get up.

I got up out of bed and quickly showered to not wake my mom up. I changed into my school uniform - a deep blue vest on top of an off-white long-sleeve top and a deep blue skirt - brushed my teeth, grabbed my bag, and headed out the door without eating anything. It was cold today, not the best day to wear a skirt. I didn't want to stay in the cold for longer than I had to, so I started speed-walking toward the school for about ten minutes until I reached the front entrance. 6:15 am like always. I sighed a breath of relief. I was comforted by the fact that I could stick to a schedule and have some sort of consistency throughout the week.

I walked into the classroom and sat in a chair near the window. This isn't my normal seat of course, but I liked sitting here the most. I apparently didn't like it enough to ask someone to move seats with me though.

I sat there near the window to look outside for a few moments. I say a few moments, but it was probably about ten minutes or so. Somehow, when you're looking at nature, time moves faster *and* slower. When I awoke from the trance I was in, I thought to myself…I didn't have any more homework, so I guess there isn't a reason anymore to come this early. Not like it mattered anyway, there were only three more days left of class. Hm…if I were to just skip the last three days, nothing would happen, right? If I leave now, no one will know I was here in the first place…Wait! Owari is probably going to come early again. What if he comes back, waits for me, and then gets upset when I'm not here anymore? I have to stay and wait for him! I can just text him asking where he is…

No. You don't have to. If he's on the way, what's the point in texting him? You're probably going to see him in like five minutes…

Five minutes passed.

I stayed in my window seat, looking outside.

Fifteen minutes passed.

I stayed in my window seat, looking outside.

Thirty minutes passed.

I stayed in my window seat, looking outside.

One hour passed.

I moved to my door seat, looking blankly in front of me as people moved past.

Two hours passed.

I stayed in my door seat, looking blankly in front of me as the teacher was lecturing.

"Miss,   can   I   the   restr   m?"

"Go ahead."

I felt a bump on my desk. It was just someone walking through the aisle to get out of the door. I blinked aggressively a couple of times to pull myself together. I looked behind me at Owari's desk to find that no one was there, turning back disappointed. It was now 8:30 am and class started a while ago. He isn't coming today.

"Miss...may I use the restroom," I said weakly as I picked up my bag with one hand, clutching my stomach with the other.

"You may."

I slowly got up from my desk and walked to the open door, quietly closing it behind me. I started walking towards the main stairwell of the school so I could go back home. As I was walking, I was looking down at the cracked, stained wooden floors that reflected a ghostly, blurry figure at me.

I was about fifteen feet away from the stairs when I heard running coming toward me. Someone was running up the stairs! I panicked; I didn't know who it was. I was too close to the stairwell at this point, there was nowhere I could duck to wait for them to pass. At this rate, if I got caught skipping class, I'd be suspended and have to do a summer course. My heart started racing and I froze five feet from the stairs. I could see who it was now.

"Owari?!"

He looked up at me, shocked to see I was standing right in front of him. "Miya!"

He was running again?

I ran down the stairwell and along the way grabbed his hand. As we reached the bottom of the stairwell, I followed through and kept running. I was getting my school shoes all dirty and didn't even pass by the lockers to get my regular shoes. The school had a massive carved-out cement path with a huge fountain in the middle of the entrance, so we ran through the cement path, past the fountain, and were now on the narrower forested path that we frequented to go home. I was breathing heavily from running, so I let go of Owari's hand to rest my hand on my waist. I dropped my bag on the ground and put my other hand on my waist and tilted slightly to the right to rest my body weight on my right leg. My breathing was steadily slowing down, so I bent down and rummaged through my bag to get out some water. I got the water, stood back up, and started drinking. As I finished, I slowly closed the cap and bent back down to put it in my bag. I put my two hands back on my waist.

"Miya?"

I heard Owari's voice from behind me. I was startled by it… I forgot I was running with him. I played it off the best I could by nonchalantly turning my head back towards him while lifting my shoulder to my chin. My mouth was slightly open because I was still breathing heavier than normal.

"Yes?" I replied.

"What's going on?" he said playfully while moving in front of me and picking up my bag to carry.

"I wanted to escape."

He had an endearing smile on his face. "I've been wanting to do that too… If you're doing the same thing for too long, pressure starts to build up and you feel the need to outdo yourself and perform well. For me, at least, this town is that pressure."

"I feel exactly the same way, Owari…" My eyes followed him intently as he was moving further away in front of me.

"I know you do Miya...so let's...escape."

"Hm?"

At this moment, my world stopped. Did he ask me to escape with him? As much as running away from school is a physical thing, when I meant 'escape', I meant in a figurative sense. I was stunned while figuring out what exactly he meant when he said this. Does he mean leave? Like, leave the town and go somewhere else? But I...Why was he late to school? Why...why was he running and...

I didn't ask him any questions, I just listened.

"I've been getting tired of doing the same old thing every day without anything to look forward to in the future. Since this is a small town, over the years we've been able to build relationships with people...and these people we've known for so long expect things from us because they think they know us...but they don't. The only people that know us are each other."

"Know...us?"

"Yes," he said as he turned around and clasped his two hands around mine. "If we were to move far away to where no one would know us, we wouldn't have any more pressure. We could be open about ourselves right from the start."

"I.."

"Let me be more blunt about this. Let's move to Tokyo together."

Those words rang in my head over and over again.

…

"Okay."

After saying this, he didn't seem to bat an eye. It's almost like he expected, without a doubt, that I'd say yes and therefore didn't think anything of it.

"Before we go, we need to do a few things first. We can't go to Tokyo without being prepared, you know?"

"I know what you mean…"

"Alright then! Shall we go?"

"Yes."

I was now following him further into the forested path without a second thought. I was hypnotized by his conviction on the matter that I couldn't have poked any holes in it even if I wanted to. This is what I've been wanting too, right? Even if I'd already been getting over my fear of judgment from people here, what better way to accelerate that process than move away entirely?

"Wait, Owari."

He stopped and turned back to me. "Yes?"

"I…need to put back my shoes."

He looked down at my shoes and noticed that I still had my school ones on. "I guess you do, huh?"

I looked down at him and apparently he had his own on already. I know he didn't have time to get them when we were in school, so he must've never put them on in the first place. He never intended to stay there.

He didn't seem mad that we were walking back. Since we went from zero-to-one hundred extremely quickly, I think we both needed to step back, now in both a figurative and literal sense…mainly to wrap our heads around what exactly we were going to do now.

   We made our way back to the school and I put my shoes away. Even though I could have just as easily stepped back into class and pretended like nothing happened, like I hadn't agreed to what I just did, it felt like we had become permanently detached from the world and could no longer return. It's almost like we *had* to leave now, there was no turning back. We made sure to be quiet when entering and exiting the building. However, while we were leaving, someone noticed us. It was Asa. We were walking out through the main entrance when Asa called out to us from the stairwell. "Owari! Wait up!" His voice wavered as he bumped down the stairs. "What're you doing?"

Even though we wanted to get out of there as soon as possible, I think Owari thought that he would have made even more of a commotion if we left without talking to him.

"We're leaving for the day," Owari said as he opened the door.

"Wait, I want to come too! I'll call Ayama to come down here as well."

Owari stopped. "She wouldn't leave class just for that."

"I didn't think Miya would have done that type of thing either, but here we are," he blurted out as he pulled out his phone, seemingly to call Ayama.

Unlike Owari who was looking outside, I was looking at Asa when he was talking to us, but after he mentioned me I turned away so he couldn't see my face. I was getting flustered. Asa noticed my now uncomfortable body language, so he apologized saying he wasn't thinking.

"Why're you so quick to call Ayama like we'll never be back? We're going to come back soon," Owari brusquely stated as he turned to look at Asa.

Asa put his phone down and turned his hand to where the screen was now facing the ceiling. "Something about what's happening right now makes it seem like you won't be back, actually," Asa said in a slightly commanding manner as he started walking toward us.

Owari didn't make an effort to move forward toward him, he just pivoted his body to where he was facing him straight on. "We will," Owari replied laconically, "just not tomorrow."

I put my head up to face Owari, confused. Where were we going tomorrow to where we could be back soon…?

"We'll be back on the last day of school, Friday."

"Mmmm.." Asa mumbled as he dropped his phone to his side and drooped his head down. "I guess I have no reason not to trust you after all." He said this like he was surrendering his pride, which from what I've heard is very uncharacteristic of him, but I guess today has just been an off day for everyone.

Owari grabbed my hand and walked me out of the door. We were about ten feet away from the door at this point, now at the cement entrance, and I looked back inside the school. Asa was running toward the door and opened it. He stayed at the entrance and yelled to us, "Make sure you're here on Friday! Remember, it's only Wednesday, so you only have two days of vacation till you're stuck with me again!"

I turned to look at Owari, awaiting his response. "I promise."

I heard the door close, and we kept walking for a few moments on the path before I stopped him. "Everything has been moving so fast. We haven't had the chance to talk about what we're going to be doing … so I'm worried."

"Don't be worried Miya, trust me a little."

"I trust you...but I do at least want to know what we're going to do until Friday, and why we can't come to class…?"

"Well, we're doing just what Asa said, we're going on vacation."

○

I woke up at 5:50 am from my phone alarm. I shut it off after the third beep, eyes still closed. I tried to stretch but was constrained by the walls around me. It was then that I realized that I hadn't fallen asleep in my bed; I fell asleep in the closet. I got my bearings, opened the closet door slightly then peered through it. I'm not exactly sure why I did this, but I suppose I wanted to check if anyone was around me. After I didn't see anyone, I opened it further and stood up. I walked into the middle of the room and looked around me like the room was foreign. Everything was so different. For some reason, it seemed so weird to be so far off the ground. Like, I wasn't the height I was supposed to be. I looked down and I was still wearing my school uniform and shoes. There was no chance that I was going to school today, so I just took them off without a second thought.

I was immediately reminded of what had happened yesterday. Seeing the cuts on my knees and feeling the bruises on my elbows as I was taking my shirt off sent me down a spiral, and I eventually fell to my knees in a lifeless pose. I sat there for a few moments, then heard a moaning noise... It was my dad. I didn't give him medicine last night, so he must be in pain. Now I was stuck between laying there for the rest of the day or getting up to help him. I chose to help him.

I didn't want to leave my room in just my underwear, so I put on a baggy black shirt and sweatpants that I only wear when I'm inside. I did my routine and got him his water and medicine from the kitchen like usual and he gradually calmed down.

Now that I was up, I figured that I should probably at least shower...but go back to sleep right after. So I did, and after, I jumped into my unmade bed face down. I turned my head to the side and took my phone out of my pocket one last time before I went to sleep. To calm me down, I read through my messages with Miya from yesterday and I remembered that I said I would come today so we could go someplace after school. I didn't want to go, but I had to go. I let so many people down yesterday, I can't do that again. And so, with that in mind, I got back up, put my now clean school uniform on, and put my shoes on. I walked out the door, down the network of paths, and made it to the school. Checking my phone, it was 8:30 am, already about an hour late. Before I walked in, I stopped outside to prepare myself for what I was about to do. Was I just going to sit there and wait for school to be over and go out with Miya then? I don't want to wait anymore. I don't want to be at school to begin with. Maybe I should just...

I opened the doors to the main hall, and once I entered I started running to the staircase. I don't know what got into me, all I knew is that I needed to get Miya and leave as soon as possible. I got up to the quarter space landing of the stairwell and was about to make my way up to the second half but was stopped in my tracks when I heard a voice yelling my name from above.

"Owari!"

"Miya!" I called back out.

I can't believe she was here. It's almost as if she knew I'd be here to get her. Out of nowhere, she started running down the staircase, and once she got to me, she grabbed my hand and booked it out of the main entrance. It couldn't be a coincidence that she was doing this; we were almost definitely on the same wavelength.

We got off of the school grounds and made it to the complex network of paths that were surrounded by forest. She stopped once we got into a wider part of the path where neighboring paths intersected.

She looked tired. Even though it was cold out, she was sweating. I couldn't tell if the sweat was just from the few-minute run we had just done, or if there was something else on her mind that made her feel that way. Either way, she went into her bag and took a sip of water just after letting go of my hand, leaning to her side to rest.

It seemed as if she was in her own world. I don't mean that in a patronizing way, she just had this natural poise and aura to her that made her seem different from everyone else. And at this moment, that aura was emanating from her stronger than I had ever seen before.

"Miya…" The name almost came out without me even thinking about it.

She turned her head to me and put her shoulder up to her chin. "Yes?"

I didn't mean to say her name, but I had to roll with it. "What's going on…?" I started moving past her and stood a few feet in front while grabbing her bag she had dropped on the ground.

She…wanted to escape? The way she said it made me certain that she didn't just mean in a physical sense… but escape from everything. She seemed a little on edge, probably because she had never done anything like this before, so I comforted her and explained that I wanted to do exactly the same thing. …This was amazing, this is exactly what I wanted. I was opening up about things I had never opened up about before, and I didn't know the next time I would have this opportunity, so I let it all out. Well, not all of it, but I opened up about wanting to get away. I knew I was right about going to school today; I just had a feeling.

Now that I had opened up to her…I didn't want this feeling of liberation to end. I took it a step further. "…Let me be more blunt about this. Let's move to Tokyo together," I said without even thinking about it. Never before had I thought of moving to Tokyo, much less now at eighteen. To my surprise though…

"Okay."

I made sure not to make it seem like a big deal. If I did, I felt as though she would panic, so I made it seem like I had this in mind from the beginning. But honestly, I was ecstatic.

We left the crossroads and after a couple more minutes of walking, she stopped and said that we were moving too fast for her and that she needed to slow down and think about what had happened. She then said that she needed to go back to school to get her shoes, but I don't think that was the only reason she wanted to go back. Along with getting her shoes, she also probably wanted to have some more time to wrap her head around everything that had taken place in the last ten minutes. I had no idea what was going through her mind beyond that, because I was too busy wrapping my *own* head around everything myself. While we were walking back, I had to come up with a plan to where we actually could move to Tokyo as painlessly as possible. After a while of thinking, I realized that it wouldn't be in our best interest to move as fast as I originally wanted to. I knew we needed to prepare, and this would obviously take time. This wasn't something where we could just move out tomorrow night even if we packed in a day. Plus, I needed to take care of a few things before we left this place for good.

She got her shoes, and we were making our way out the door when Asa stopped us. Usually, I'd humor him, but I wasn't in the mood to. We talked to him for a while, convincing him not to follow us out of the school. When we were leaving, he said that we were going on vacation or something…and that gave me an idea.

I heard the door close, and we kept walking for a few seconds; now back on the forested paths.

"Wait, Owari." She stopped and tugged on my arm. "Everything has been moving so fast. We haven't had the chance to talk about what we're going to be doing…so I'm worried."

"Don't be worried Miya, trust me a little."

"I trust you…but I do at least want to know what we're

going to do until Friday, and why we can't come to class.."

"Well, we're doing just what Asa said, we're going on vacation."

"...Vacation?"

"Mh-mmm. Vacation." I reached my shivering hand out, signaling to hold hers. She grabbed it and we started moving again. "Yeah, we're going to move to Tokyo, but we deserve something for getting past high school right? And we need our diplomas, so we're coming back on Friday to receive them."

The tension loosened a little and we were back to playful banter. "Diplomas? Can you even get yours? You missed like ninety-nine percent of the school days," she noted, laughing.

I laughed too. "Attendance isn't compulsory at our school. All we need to do is pass our classes.

"You've been doing the assignments?"

"No, I haven't…but all the assignments are posted on the school website under our teacher's name, remember?"

"Oooh, right…"

"So all I'm required to do is complete the minimum number of assignments needed to get a passing grade and turn them in before Friday. You can turn them in online, so we don't need to go back until then."

"I'm glad to hear that…" she said in a sentimental tone as she looked down.

"Don't worry, everything is going to turn out just fine."

"I know it will…" There was a couple of seconds pause before she continued. "Oh! So where are we going on vacation?" she asked with a beaming smile as she tugged on my arm, turning her head to me in anticipation.

"Hm…well it can't be somewhere too far since we have to come back here in a couple of days…"

"And you have to do your assignments, so we can't go somewhere where we wouldn't have time to relax and do it."

"Oh yeah, you're right… I completely forgot about having to do that already."

She made a sarcastic yet compassionate face. "Yeah… what a vacation…doing homework."

I laughed. "I won't be doing it the whole time…maybe just a day. And you're there to help me…so we'll get through it faster."

She smiled but tried to hide it with her right hand.

"Anyways, how's a ryokan sound? One with an onsen

too."

"That sounds amazing!!" she exclaimed. "I've never been to one before~"

"I haven't either, so it'll be really fun to experience that for the first time together...Not many people our age get to go because it's more expensive than a regular hotel."

"I was just about to say...we don't really have the money for it since we don't work."

"I have the money for it, no worries."

"Whaa~? How? You didn't steal it, did you?"

We turned right on the path. "Of course not. Even though my dad isn't working either, we get checks from Sano every month because my dad owns a percentage of the company."

"I completely forgot about Sano. And since it's the biggest electronics company in Japan, it must be a huge sum of money, right?"

"You'd think that, but he just owns a tiny percentage. He never actually worked for the company; I think my grandfather just gave him a percentage out of principle for being part of the family I guess?"

"Mh..."

"And the medicine he has is expensive, so a large portion of that income we get goes straight into that, and he has some debts to pay off as well... So it's not that much after all the expenses."

"So will we have enough to do everything we want to?" she asked as she moved her eyebrows up slightly.

"I don't use the extra money for anything, and neither does he, so it just gets piled up there. It's enough for a ryokan, but probably not enough to move to Tokyo..."

"Should we not go anywhere then and use all the money to go to Tokyo?"

"Nah, we deserve this... We'll figure it out," I replied in a hopeful tone while walking up to my doorstep. "I'll get everything I need to pack and then we'll head to your house and get everything you need."

"Okay~"

I let go of her hand and started opening the door, taking my shoes off before I entered. "Do you want to come inside or stay out here?"

Her eyes lit up. "It's pretty cold, so I'll come inside."

"Okay, just take your shoes off before you come in."

"Mhm!" she said, lifting her right leg vertically behind

her and taking off one shoe before doing the same thing with the other.

I opened the door and let her walk in first. She stepped to the side to not crowd the doorway and give me enough space to enter. Closing the door behind us, I held her hand again and led her to my room. "Oh, crap…I forgot I didn't clean it up this morning."

The room was very messy. Luckily this morning I cleaned up the broken lamp and fallen pills in the living room, but I hadn't cleaned my room at all since I messed it up last night. Clothes were on the floor, the bed was unmade, books that were once neatly put on shelves were on the floor, and my school bag's contents were spread out everywhere around the closet.

"Pretty rough night last night, so the room got a little messed up," I said as I let go of her hand and started picking up my clothes off of the floor.

"Is everything okay?" she asked as she put her bag on the chair next to my desk while curiously looking around.

"Yeah, everything's fine. Something just happened yesterday that sent me in a bit of disarray."

"Something happened?"

I started to make my bed. "Oh yeah, but I don't want to talk about it right now. I'll tell you about it later though, promise."

"Okay, no worries, as long as it isn't too bad I guess I don't need to know right away~" she said, sitting down on my bed while rocking her feet after I finished making it.

"It isn't," I said, now moving to the bookshelf.

That was the biggest lie I've probably ever told. It was bad. But I couldn't say that right now. It was at that moment when it hit me, that the reason I was so eager to leave was probably because I wanted to get away from anything that reminded me of what happened yesterday. My face started to get red; I wanted to stop thinking about it as soon as possible.

"One second Miya."

"No worries~"

I stepped out of the room with clothes in my arm to change into my regular clothes in the bathroom. Since it was cold, I put on a reflective black bomber jacket on top of a plain black shirt with beige aviation pants with straps on them. When I was done changing, I walked back into my room.

"Speaking of yesterday, how was yours?"

"You know what, it was surprisingly good. It's weird

actually; I don't like school because of all the people around, but I don't like being at home because of how disconnected I feel."

"Well, it's only your mom at home with you, right? And from what you've told me, you don't interact with her that much, so I could see how anyone in your situation would feel disconnected. Sometimes I do too."

"True, but aren't I weird for that? Like...why can't I be satisfied...I should be able to be comfortable with a lot of people or none at all, shouldn't I? What does it mean if I don't like either?"

"That's not weird in the slightest. In my opinion, what you're describing is the most normal, and everyone else is weird. What you enjoy is just being with a few people who you really like and that's when you're most comfortable...what's wrong with that?"

"Huh, when you put it plainly like that, it does seem normal."

"See?" I responded sympathetically as I finished everything on the bookshelf and moved to the closet.

○

Emotions are not valued in the slightest. Take for example when someone asks how your day is:

"Hey, how're you doing?"
"I'm doing great, how about you?"
"Good to hear, I haven't been doing that well recently."
"What's been going on?"

Did you catch that? We only ask someone to elaborate when they've been doing worse than 'normal'. From this, one would conclude that negative emotions are valued more than positive ones, but that's not the case either. Oftentimes, even if we are going through a rough patch in our lives, we feel as though we *have to* act happy to outsiders. From that, the logical conclusion would be that people value positive emotions more than negative ones, but we've come to conflicting solutions now. Both situations cannot be the case. So, what is the solution to this dilemma? What emotions are valued more? Positive, or negative?

Continuing my point, people don't often want to say they're doing worse than normal because they don't want to have to elaborate, but if we had to elaborate, no matter if you were doing better or worse, we'd be more comfortable sharing when we are feeling down. We *have to* act happy on the surface, but we elaborate when we're sad. This conflict makes people want to shut off all of their emotions as there is virtually no winning.

You should either value all emotions equally, or value none at all. Before I said that emotions aren't valued at all, but this is not technically the case. What we have is a faux value. We put a faux value on emotions but don't do it to the point where we need to reach our full potential. It is often thought that no one *really* cares how others feel, that they just put this faux value on other people's emotions either out of societal pressure, or for the other person to reciprocate those feelings back to them when they need it, but I care. In fact, you will find that I'm one of the only people who genuinely care about how others feel.

◯

"So, are you ready to go?" I said, grabbing my large maroon duffle bag that was now filled with clothes.

"Yess. Oh, by the way, your room looks a lot bigger when it's all cleared up like this."

I looked around the room. "Since this is your first time seeing it cleared up, I guess it would," I said as I reached my hand out.

We walked out of my room, through the living room, and out the door now back on the paths. Miya lived in an apartment complex closer to the city, so she was directing me toward the complex since I am largely unfamiliar with the area.

"Right here~ Left here~ Oh! There's a shortcut down this alley, we should go through there."

And there we were, standing outside of her apartment complex. It was a monsterous gray building with hundreds of windows with balconies on each one. It didn't look run down, but it didn't look like it was in its prime either. There was an entranceway in the middle of the complex with a bright red awning over it. The entranceway was a long hallway that connected to all of the first-floor rooms, but Miya's apartment was on the fifth floor, so we had to take the flight upstairs at the back of the hallway. As I was walking through the hallway, moving past all the rooms, I noticed something… It was quiet. All of the parking spaces were filled, but there was no noise coming from any of the rooms. And since it was an urban area, there were no sounds of nature such as trees swaying in the wind or birds chirping. I could see how someone would feel disconnected here.

We walked up to the third floor and stopped to look out one of the windowed spaces on the wall. I looked, and I saw complex corridors and buildings that were seemingly all connected to a grid. There weren't many people out since it was early in the morning on a Wednesday… so it looked lifeless despite the contemporary scenery.

"Do you like this type of view?" Miya asked, breaking the silence.

"Hmm…are you talking about the city view? Opposed to looking outside your window and seeing a lake or the woods or something?"

"Yeah…It, uhm, gets pretty tiring to look at it every day, but I think that if all I was exposed to was nature, I'd find the city fascinating, so I can't complain that much. Although, since I have lived in the city my whole life, I would like some change."

I looked at her. "Well, in Tokyo, there's even less green…so what're we going to do about that?"

She looked at me. "We can start a garden," she said, looking back outside the open space in the wall. "We can start a garden from the ground up...and the plants will mature along with us. Once they're fully grown, it'll mark the point where we've grown fully accustomed to the new life that awaits us."

"That sounds like a perfect idea." And to be honest, it was. A garden was the last thing on my mind.

We continued ascending the stairs to the fifth floor and walked over to the middle of the hallway to her door. She let go of my hand and bent down to the floor to get a key that was hidden under the entrance mat, picking it up to unlock the door. No one was home since her mom was at work.

Her house was about the same size as mine, just more modern. As we walked in, she told me the layout of the house. The entrance was a long hallway that connected to all the rooms. The first room on the right was her bedroom, and the first room on the left was her mother's bedroom. Further down the hall on the right was a room that opened up to an office space that also functioned as a guest bedroom, and past her mother's bedroom on the left was a bathroom. Past the hallway, it expanded from a narrow space to a huge room. On the right was the living area, and on the left was the kitchen. The floors glistened a shiny light brown colored wood and the walls were white.

We went to her room and once we opened the door I was amazed to find out that the room was fully customized to her style. I had never seen anything like this. As you enter, you're met with a large white bookshelf on the left and the right expanded to the rest of her room. The walls had been covered in a pastel pink wallpaper with framed art plastered all over it from her favorite artists. In the back right corner, there was her bed, filled with pillows and plushies of her favorite characters. On the bookcase, the top two shelves were lined with manga, novels, and Blu-ray disks of her favorite movies. In the space in front of them, there were small figures from the series on the bookshelves. On the middle bookshelf, there were larger figures and more art from her favorite artists; some were even signed. On the bottom two shelves, there was her music collection. She had vinyl records and CDs from all her favorite musicians. The main lights were off in her room, but she had LED strip lights around the ceiling line colored purple. The light brown wooden floors connected from the rest of the house to her room, but she put in a small pink rug with one of her favorite characters on it. I wasn't sure who it was, but it was cute. In the right corner closest to us, she had a small white desk that had been styled to look like something from the Victorian era. On it was a small desk lamp and stacks of notebooks that had been neatly arranged in a small cubby on the desk. Next to the desk was a keyboard piano with a small swivel stool tucked under it. My room was nothing like this, I was kind of jealous.

"Woah…your room looks amazing…I never knew you were into stuff like this."

She walked past the bookshelf to her closet which filled the left wall. To the right of the closet was a door that led to her personal bathroom. "Aaaah thank you! I've spent a lot of time curating it to my taste."

"And money…"

"I guess so, but it's not like I got all this stuff overnight, it's taken a while for me to get everything.

As she walked forward, I stayed in the doorway and turned to the bookshelf. "Do you mind?"

"Of course not, go ahead."

Once she gave me the go-ahead, I picked up a random book and started flipping through it. I had never heard of this before... I looked at everything else on the top few bookshelves, but I only recognized a few of the movies and manga she had, but everyone knew those. I put the book back that I had gotten out and then bent down to look at her music. As I was looking, I could hear her humming to herself while she was rummaging around in her closet looking for clothes to put in her bag; it was a joyful melody. When I finished looking through the CDs and records, I moved over to her bed and sat down on it, placing my bag next to me.

I looked into her closet and saw a huge expansion of clothes. Since we'd only been with each other at school up to this point, I had never seen her wear anything but her uniform, so I was curious to see everything she had. She had a neverending amount of skirts, dresses, tops, shoes, and a million different accessory items. The styles of everything varied to the Y2K fashion trend, which was making a comeback, a more western streetwear style, a sophisticated look, punk, and everything in between. There were tight clothes, baggy clothes, different materials, tons of jewelry, and anything else you could think of.

"You have so many clothes...and it all looks so good!"

"I knoww. Thank you. It sucks because I never have

the opportunity to wear them all that much, but I'm really into fashion."

"I can tell...it all looks amazing and I'm sure it looks really good on you."

"Thank you!" She kept picking things up to put in her bag. "Can you turn around for a sec?"

"Mhm," I said as I turned around and looked in the direction of her desk. I could hear her shuffling and heard the sound of clothes moving.

"Okay, you can turn back around."

I turned to her again and she had changed outfits! She no longer had her school uniform on, she had something completely different. She had put on thigh-high socks that reached past her knees on top of fishnet leggings and had on an oversized black graphic t-shirt with one of her favorite bands that slightly hid light blue denim cut-off shorts underneath. She also had put on a velvet black choker and silver earrings that dangled down from her ears. "How do I look?" she asked as she spun around.

Never once had I felt star-struck until now. "You look amazing...I never want to see you in your school uniform again!" I said while running up to hug her. I closed my eyes and smiled.

"Trust me, I don't either, I much prefer this." I could hear her smile through how she talked.

We let go and I put my two hands on her shoulders: our eyes locked. "Wait, but, you're going to be really cold."

She turned to her closet. "Don't worry, I'm going to bring a jacket."

I let go of her so she could bring out the jacket she was talking about; it was a black leather jacket that reflected a purple hue from the lights. I could tell it would be an oversized fit on her, it was longer than her already oversized shirt.

"Ready to go?~"

"Uh-huh."

We left her room after she turned off the LED lights with a small remote. She had blackout curtains, so it was pitch black once they were turned off. We closed the door behind us and made our way to the entrance where I put my shoes back on. Meanwhile, Miya had reached into the cabinet at the entrance and brought out long leather boots that reached just below her knee. We opened the front door, locked it, put the key under the mat, and made our way down the stairs.

I couldn't believe it. We were really going on vacation,

just the two of us. This is the first time I've ever done something like this. I turned my head to Miya, who was holding her leather jacket in one arm, holding her travel bag in the other, and toting a small black bag over her shoulder. Never before had I seen her like this...I wasn't going to take it for granted.

We got to the front of the apartment complex and she put on her jacket. I held out my arm and we interlocked them.

"Hey," she said gently, turning her head to mine. "How far away is the ryokan again?"

"Oh, it's about an hour from here. So not *too* far, but far enough to feel like a real vacation."

"Perfect! So, do you have a car?"

"No...do you?"

"No..."

We both paused for a moment and I turned my head to her, eyes widened. "So how're we going to get there?"

Chapter 2B

Chapter 2B:
The Occurrence

Picture this, you develop romantic feelings toward your friend. You now have two choices: you can either confess or stay silent. Let's weigh out your options. When you stay silent, there is a zero percent chance that you will go out with them. If you confess, there's always a chance for the person to reciprocate your feelings, even if the chance is minuscule. So, why are people so afraid to confess these feelings to others? Well, when laying it out as I have, it seems illogical not to. However, most people are afraid that if the person they're going to confess to will not reciprocate their feelings, it could mess up the friendship they have. This could be the case, but if you like the person so much that you're willing to take the chance to mess up your friendship to further your once platonic relationship into a romantic one, the choice seems like a no-brainer. If you aren't willing to confess, then that romantic relationship probably wouldn't have worked out in the end anyway. Let me paraphrase something interesting I read in a book once:

"Love is irrational, it makes you do irrational things.
People often marry the person they love.
Therefore, marrying the person you love is irrational.
You should marry someone you *don't* love for the best results."

Although this way of thinking is irrational itself and no one would ever follow this, it made me think about what would really make the best partner. In the case of marrying someone, love cannot simply be the only reason you marry. People in love can fight. People in love can disagree on crucial things that make a relationship work. People in love can hate each other by the end of it. This is disheartening but true. To go back; love, empathy, openness, and the ability to compromise, are just a few of the things that people need to be able to have a successful long-term relationship. You can't be exactly the same, but you can't be too dissimilar either; there's a long list of things that people need to make a relationship work. I don't mean moronic standards such as a height or weight requirement, I'm merely talking about a list of concepts in a person. It's safe to say that I have found the perfect person to meet all of these concepts, and I couldn't be happier about it.

○

"Umm...could we take the train?" she said as she started to walk aimlessly in front of me.

"We have no way to get to the station..." I turned my head to the side and looked down.

"Oh..."

"Yeah."

Miya started making a noise. I looked up to see what was wrong...but she was clutching her stomach and laughing. She was laughing so hard she couldn't breathe for a second.

"Hey! What's so funny?"

She traced the bottom of her eye with her fingertip,

rubbing off the tears that came out from laughing. "It's funny how serious you were. It's not a big deal, I was just messing with you."

I began to get a little flustered and put my hands in my jacket's pockets. "Well…I…"

She pulled out her phone from her back pocket and started putting in a phone number I didn't recognize. She hit the call button and as it started ringing she put her phone screen in my direction to show me who she was calling. "I'm calling a taxi."

My eyes widened and my face went blank. I was so dumb not to think we could've just called a taxi this whole time. I moved my head up and to the left and took my hands out of my pockets to cross my arms along my chest. "Well…I knew we could've called a taxi this whole time of course, but I didn't know if you'd be comfortable with it…"

She walked closer to me, up till she was about an inch away, looked in my eyes and made an impish smile, the phone still ringing. "There was a psychology study that said that people tend to look up and right when trying to recall something, but they look up and left when lying about recalling something. Interesting, right?" The person on the line picked up and she walked away from me, purposefully swinging her hair in my face. "Helloo~?"

"Aah!" I blurted out, backing away and moving my hand to my face. "Why'd you-"

She turned around quickly on her heels and put her finger up to her mouth. She smiled that same impish smile again. "Yeah, that works."

I let loose and started to smile.

"Fifteen minutes? No worries." … "M-hm. See you soon."

"It'll be fifteen minutes before they get here?"

"Yep, fifteen minutes," she said, walking to the curb and sitting down on it. I walked over and sat next to her.

○

Today was special. It was the first time I had ever been in Owari's room before, much less his house. I wonder what it was that happened that made his room so messy. Not that I mind, but it was quite worrying. My first thought was that he fought with someone, but he didn't have any visible bruises on his face or hands or anything, so that can't be the case. I'm not sure what else could have happened, but he said he'd tell me later…so there's no point in wondering I suppose. Anyways, I wasn't sure what I was expecting, but the books he reads are mostly non-fiction. Not retelling of history or encyclopedia-type books, but books like "The Philosophy of Aristotle" and biographies and teachings of former Japanese Emperors. He also had some fiction from the likes of Murakami and other classic authors, but either way, it was really interesting to see what he liked to read for fun. The stereotype of people who read philosophy books is that they can't let loose, are serious, and only talk about philosophy, but he isn't like that at all. I think that he just enjoys viewing other people's perspectives on things, and that's a good quality in a person. Anyways, he seemed equally as fascinated looking at my bookshelf and my personal tastes in media. I think I'm going to bring some manga series to Tokyo that I think he might enjoy - I know he'd be open to it. I guess we had never talked about our interests in books or movies or anything like that. It makes me wonder what exactly we did talk about when we first became friends.

On another note, we've had a lot of physical displays of affection, which is new to me. No one had ever held my hand or hugged me or anything else, so it felt really, really nice. I'm glad he's been equal in returning the affection, it makes me feel wanted and cared for, even if we're just friends. We've been moving so fast - I wouldn't be surprised if we started dating soon. You know what, I'm going to set it in stone! If by the end of Friday he doesn't ask me to be his girlfriend, then I'll ask him! I can't be afraid anymore; I can't go back on it now. Wish me luck!

Oh!!! How could I forget? He finally saw me in clothes that weren't my school uniform! That was really exciting too. I think I expected him to dress how I thought he would (lol) but he seemed surprised by what I had on, and he'll definitely be more surprised when he sees the other outfits I brought on the trip. I also brought some makeup on the trip, and I'm going to start doing it more often. I'm also going to try to style my hair differently more often as well - I think that since moving to Tokyo is such a big change, I've been inspired to change in a lot of other ways too. I'm also very much looking forward to the big new city life - I think it'll inspire my writing in more ways than I could be conscious of. Thank you for this opportunity!!

I closed my notebook and put the pen in the spiral.

○

About five minutes passed and I was starting to get impatient. I know the driver said that he'd be fifteen minutes, so I shouldn't be surprised, but…well… There is no but, I was bored. Normally we'd be talking, but I think she was fatigued from the initial adrenaline rush that was the last three hours. Without warning, I felt something hit me. I turned to my right and her head was laying on my shoulder, eyes closed. It's safe to say that I wasn't bored anymore. How could I be with Miya there next to me? Suddenly this intense, exhilarating feeling rushed through my body, and I had a huge smile on my face. So huge that my face muscles started to hurt. I can't take Miya for granted, I thought to myself. The intense initial feeling sizzled out after a few minutes, but I still had a smile on my face. I moved my shoulder and wrapped my right arm around Miya's, leaning my head on hers. After that, ten minutes passed like nothing.

I found that I closed my eyes at some point in the ten

minutes because soon after I was startled by a tap on my shoulder. An old man stood in front of me, bent down to eye level.

"Were you the one who called the taxi?"

I brought my head back up and shook Miya a little to wake her up. "Miya, Miya, the driver's here."

She lifted her head up and slowly opened her eyes. When she did, she put her hand over them to block the sunlight. She stretched a little to wake herself up, looking at me with an unconcerned look. "What'd you say?"

I turned my head to the driver.

"Hmn?" She followed suit and turned her head in the direction I had turned to.

"Taxi?" he said, getting up.

Her eyes enlarged. "Oh!" She got up quickly and brushed herself off from the dirt on the curb. "Yes, I was the one who called. Thank you for coming," she said quickly while bowing.

She seemed to reset almost. Being that we were alone for a while, I forgot she wasn't her animated self around people she was unfamiliar with; she gets nervous. For a split second, I was confused, but when I remembered, I understood. She told me once that she has a hard time gauging how friendly to act toward new people in her life. Because of this, she appears distant at first, but once she gets a feel for the other person, she becomes comfortable around them. Either way, I wasn't going to make it a big deal to her. Not just for her sake, but also because I truly didn't mind.

"Are you ready to go, or do you need more time?"

"I'm ready to go, are you?"

I got up. "Yep."

We walked over to the car and put our bags in the trunk. After that, we made our way to the back seat and sat down.

"So, where to?"

We said the location of the ryokan and he started typing in the address on his GPS. We strapped our seatbelts and looked at each other in anticipation while he continued to type.

"Huh? Is this right?"

"Is something wrong?" she asked, turning her gaze to the driver's seat.

"It says the ryokan is an hour away… maybe I typed in the wrong address."

She looked back at me with a concerned look on her face. "N-No... That's the correct address." She turned back to him and pointed at the location on his GPS. "It's an hour away."

He turned back to us. "You do know how much this is going to cost, right?"

She turned back to me. "Well, yeah. Around 30,000 yen, right?"

"R-Right. Okay. Well then." He clicked 'Confirm' on his GPS. "We'll be on our way momentarily."

"Okay."

"Thank you."

He shifted gears to 'D' and set off in the direction the GPS took him. We had a pretty quiet ride there except for the occasional small talk from the driver. We both gazed out the window at the passing trees for most of the ride. The hour definitely felt like its length while we were driving, but afterward it all kind of blended together so it didn't seem long at all.

We arrived at the ryokan, got out of the car, and went to the trunk to get our bags when the driver got out. He looked anxious.

"Is something the matter, sir?"

"It's just that…you both are so young so it's hard to believe you have that much to spend on a cab. I don't want you running off without paying…"

"No worries, I understand," I said as I set my bag on the ground and took my wallet out of my pocket, taking out my card. "Do you take debit?"

"I-I do. One moment please," he nervously said as he went back in his car, dangling his legs out almost horizontally, looking for his card reader.

After about thirty seconds of rummaging inside, he finally found it. Once he was done looking, I walked up to him and inserted the card into the reader. He was looking at the screen intensely, I suppose to make sure that the purchase was valid, when we heard a 'ding!' sound emitting from the reader. On the screen, it read 'Accepted!' with bright green text.

"Huh…" he murmured to himself.

I put the card back in my wallet but took something else out in its place. The light reflected off the object blinded me for a second, but when I could see clearly again I looked at him and he was in his car once more, putting the card reader back in a more convenient spot.

I walked closer to the driver's car door and silently stood there waiting for him to pop back up. Once he was finished putting it back in its proper place, he tried to turn around, but I was so close to the door that he couldn't do it all the way and was startled by how close I was.

"Ah! Eh..e-excus-"

CHNK

I suppose Miya heard this sound, so she inquired about it, moving closer to me. "Hmn? What was that sound?"

Blood slowly trickled down his body and eventually made its way to the pavement.

"How do you like that?" I thought, peering into his now lifeless gray eyes. "Now do you think that I'm just some lowly high schooler who can't pay for anything and will steal from someone like you? How could you think so poorly of me? I'm hurt."

I never said any of this aloud because his heart already stopped, but I played the scene out in my head. His body dropped to the ground in an instant, carrying the knife lodged in his chest with him. Blood was spewing out of his mouth and his white collared shirt had turned red.

Once he dropped, Miya started screaming, "Owari??

What did you just do!?"

I turned around expecting Miya to be grateful for what I had just accomplished, but her face was filled with tears; her eyes filled with terror.

"Huh…" he murmured to himself.

I put the card back in my wallet and thought to myself, "Mn...I just had the weirdest thought play out just now..." I shook my head, brushed it off, and continued the transaction. "Is that all there is left to do?"

"Y-Yes sir," he said bowing. "Thank you for your patronage." He quickly got back into the car, I assume without checking his GPS, because he was driving the wrong way once he left the parking lot.

I turned around back in the direction of Miya to get my bag, but while I was talking to the driver she had already picked it up without me knowing. Miya held her right arm out horizontally with the bag in hand, a huge smile on her face. "Here you go."

"Thank you very much." I smiled back. "Shall we go in?"

"M-hm!"

We started walking in tandem to the front entrance of the ryokan. When the doors opened, we were greeted by a large, spacious room that was entirely made from wood. The floors, walls, ceiling, desks, chairs, everything. It was all made of wood. In the center of this huge room, there was a massive rug that was in front of a wood-powered fireplace surrounded by couches and chairs. I didn't do enough research on the place we were staying, so I didn't know if it was so old that it was always like this, or if it was a new establishment trying to imitate an old style, but either way, it felt cozy. To the right was a front desk with a receptionist behind it.

She stood up and greeted us with a bow. "Hello, welcome to Izumi Inn. Do you have a reservation with us?"

"Hi, yes," I said, walking closer to the desk. "The reservation is under the name Sano."

Miya pulled me to the side after walking up. "You made a reservation?!" she whispered.

I whispered back. "Yeah. This place requires it. Plus, I wanted to make sure we got a good room…"

"Here are two keys to your room," she said, placing two keys in my hand and pulling us back into the conversation.

I passed the other one to Miya and she continued to give us a rundown of the features of the ryokan we were staying at. "Do you need an attendant to help you find the way to your room?"

"We're okay. Thank you, ma'am."

"Okay. Just call down to the reception desk if you need anything."

"We will," I said, walking in the direction of our room.

Once we made it to our room, I unlocked the door and it expanded to an also massive space. The room had two six-tatami rooms side by side with a sliding screen divider in the middle. On the far tatami-mat room side was a low wooden table with six seats. In the closer room were two beds with a nightstand separating them. The walls to our left were pastel green, and on them hung classical Japanese art in wooden frames. On the walls that weren't green, there was a huge window that spanned the entire wall. I placed my bag down on my bed and walked over to the window to peer outside, eager to look at the view. Outside was a beautiful green gorge with a small stream running throughout. Closer to our room, however, was the onsen. It was closed off from the wilderness by wooden vinyl fences and a cement floor surrounding the bath. The sheer heat from the water fogged up the windows in our room a little bit. I looked back to where I thought Miya was, near the beds, but there she was, right next to me, also peering down to the onsen.

"I've never been to an onsen before..."

"Really? Even I have... and I never do anything."

She rolled her eyes. "Woww, what is that supposed to mean?" she said while laughing.

I laughed too but covered my mouth. "Sorry~"

She turned back to the window. "So, is it private? Or is it a public to everyone in the ryokan?"

"There's a bigger, free public one that anyone in the ryokan can use, but there are smaller private ones like the one you see down there."

"You got a private one?!"

"Yeah, duh. This is our vacation; I don't want to share that with anyone."

"That's sweet of you. Well, do you want to go?!"

"Whatt?" I replied in a higher-pitched tone while walking from the window to the bed. "I'm tired." I flopped my back on the bed, closing my eyes like I was sleeping.

"You know you landed on your bag, right?"

"I-I know. And it hurts so much."

I could hear her walking over to me while laughing. Once she got next to my bed, she pulled the bag out from under me and dropped it on the floor. Now that the bag was on the floor and I was lying flat on my back, she hopped on the bed with me and got on top of me in a vajrasana pose on my lower legs.

I opened my eyes back up slightly, curious as to what she was doing.

"Don't you want to go?" she let out with a played-up frown.

"*I 'm s l e e p i n g g g,*" I whispered back.

Her face turned from a sad expression to one that looked annoyed. "I can see your eyes open."

As soon as she said that I shut my eyes again. I smiled slightly but couldn't hold it in after a couple of seconds. I laughed and picked my upper body up so we were at the same eye level, putting my arms back with the palms of my hands on the bed to support me. When I got up, she got off of my legs but still sat on my bed next to me. She was laughing too.

She started talking in her excited tone. "So, can we go yet?" she asked again while putting down her fists on her thighs repeatedly in excitement.

I looked out the window. "It's still bright outside. People don't usually do outdoor onsens until it's dark out. Gives it more of an atmospheric vibe, you know?"

"Oh, really?" she brought her pointer finger up to her chin and curled it under. "I guess that makes sense..."

"I promise we'll go after we've had dinner, okay?"

"Kay!" she said, hopping off my bed and looking into her bag that was on the adjacent one.

I lay back down on my back and stared at the ceiling. "That was...a really weird thought earlier," I said to myself. I turned to Miya, who was still searching through her bag. "...I wonder what Miya would think of me if she knew I thought that... Never mind what happened today, I wonder what Miya would think if I told her about what happened yesterday." My mind kept racing and my stomach turned. Ughh. I turned my gaze to the ceiling again.

"Owari? Owarrii?" Miya was waving her hand in front of my face. "Are you there?"

"Huh? Oh! Hey Miya, what's up?"

"Are you okay? It seems like your head is in the clouds somewhere," she said, turning her head diagonally with empathy.

I got up again, this time out of bed fully. "Yeah, I'm okay. Something just popped into my mind and I got a little distracted."

"Oh. What was it…?"

"Well…"

"If you don't want to say it's okay."

"I want to tell you but it's hard right now."

"Okay, if you want, I'll give you a second to think it over, and then if you find the courage we can talk about it, kay?"

"Okay, thank you, Miya." I walked over to the window again and peered outside. I wondered if I should tell her. After all…thoughts aren't the same things as actions. It doesn't matter if you think something like that for a split second, because if you know you'll never actually do it, then…

But I did do it. I did it to that kid.

I turned around quickly and walked over to Miya, I decided I should tell her. Before I could back out, I instantly started saying what was on my mind. "Earlier, I…when I was paying with the card…this intrusive thought came into my mind."

"Intrusive thought? What was it?"

"I had this random thought that like…if I suddenly walked up to the driver, I could have stabbed and killed him with a knife I had in my pocket."

"Hmm…Okay."

"Do you hate me now?"

She smiled. "Of course not. Everyone gets thoughts like those. Plus, do you even have a knife in your pocket?"

I laughed a little. "No, I don't." I really didn't have a knife, but realizing I was worrying like I actually could've stabbed him at that very moment seemed stupid now.

"See? Even if you wanted to stab him, you couldn't have, so there's no need to worry. It'd be a slightly different thing if you did have a knife and thought about it, but you didn't, so there's no need to worry."

"What if I did have a knife then?"

She looked a little confused. "Do you?"

"No, no. I promise. I just wonder what you would've thought…or rather…how it'd be different if I did."

"I'd have no reason not to be fine with it as you didn't do anything Owari. It's o-kay. Everyone has these thoughts, sometimes people have them multiple times a day. It doesn't mean a single thing, at least to me."

"Okay..."

"Let's think about this another way, what if I confided in you and said *I* was thinking about stabbing him. Well, scratch that, I *DID* think about stabbing him at one point during the trip."

Now I was the one who looked surprised. "You did?!"

"Nope. But you wouldn't have known even if I did, right? So what's the difference between me, someone who didn't think it, and you, someone who did?"

"Nothing's different at all..." I looked down.

"Nothing's different at all!~" she repeated back to me, clasping her hands together, agreeing. "Do you feel a little better now?"

I looked back up at her and smiled, "I do Miya, thank you a lot. How did you know exactly what to say to make me feel better so effortlessly?"

"I just say whatever I'd want to hear. And since I know all of the things I said just now to be true. Whenever I have any intrusive thoughts like that I just kind of think, 'Woah lol that was weird', and move on. And now that I've told you what I do, whenever in the future you have thoughts like that, you can just laugh to yourself and say, 'Woah lol that was weird.'"

"Woah..lol that was weird," I laughed a little to myself as I said it out loud.

She laughed too. "See, doesn't it make you feel better?"

"It does."

"I'm glad. Anyways, what do you want to do until later?"

"I see you're still stuck on the onsen - well... Before we go, we should eat something. It's already 4:00 pm, so we might as well just settle down and wait until dinner."

"Okay~"

It was now 6:00 pm and we were called by the receptionist down the hall saying that our food was being prepared, and we would have to wait for another ten to fifteen minutes. At a ryokan, they serve a traditional multi-course meal that comes in waves that are usually prepared with some type of alcohol. But since we're both only eighteen, they couldn't serve it to us, so we'll just have to live with the regular meals. On another note, in the two hours while we were waiting, I remembered that in the closet there were yukatas we could wear. Ryokan's always have complimentary yukata that allow the customer to embrace the traditional lifestyle that they're trying to emulate. So, during the two-hour time period, we put them on to embrace tradition. On top of looking amazing, well, at least on Miya, they were a lot more comfortable than regular clothes. It'd be too odd to wear these out in public, but even so, I wish I could wear them all the time. Fifteen minutes had passed from the initial call and multiple waiters walked in without even knocking. Miya and I were laying down on our respective beds, talking while waiting, but when they came in we jolted up and watched them bring out bowls of never-ending food onto the low table in the room divided by the now scrunched-up screen.

The waiters finished placing everything on the table and eventually left the room. They told us that whenever we wanted the next set of dishes, all we had to do was call the reception desk and tell them the room number.

"All of this looks amazing!~" Miya's eyes sparkled as she sat down.

"It really does, I'm blown away." I sat down too.

"Oh um...it's all fish."

"What, you don't like seafood?"

"I don't think I like seafood *this* much, but it looks too good to pass up."

We ate everything in about fifteen minutes and then called the receptionist to get our second round of food.

"So there's even more food coming after this second round?!"

"Yeah. This is sort of an appetizer."

Her jaw dropped slightly. "Is this the second appetizer then?" she jokingly asked. "I don't know if I can eat all this if there are even more waves coming."

"No one can," I said as I raised my fist and closed my eyes. "But we must because we don't want to upset the old lady who cooked this."

"Are you for real?" she responded in a deadpan voice.

I opened one eye and put down my fist. "Hm? Was I not convincing?"

"Uhm. No."

"Well, I *was* kidding...but on a serious note..*do* you really want to upset the old lady who cooked this?" She stared blankly at me for a couple of seconds before I started laughing. "It doesn't matter, she nor anyone else cares how much you eat. Just eat what you want. It would be good to save some room for the stuff coming soon though."

She giggled and continued eating.

Four more waves came in one after another. We were now on the dessert of sorts, and I could tell Miya was getting sick from eating everything. So was I.

"I-Is this the last one?" Miya said weakly.

"Yes," I responded with the same intensity.

We finished eating the dessert and the waiters came in one last time to take our bowls away. When they were leaving, they thanked us and told us to have a nice night.

"I've never eaten that much at one time in my life," I said, laying down on my back on the pillow-esk seat we were sitting on.

She did the same across from me. "I don't think I've had that much in my life combined period."

We both laughed, but it was a painful laugh.

"Oh, and guess what?"

"What?"

"We get to do this every morning and every evening." I waited a few moments after I said this, but she didn't respond. I was worried, so I got up to check on her from the other side of the table and she looked dead.

"Are you dead?"

"Yes."

"Me too," I huffed, laying back down.

…

I opened my eyes, and it was completely dark in the room beside a few lights outside and another light in the corner of my eye. I guess I had fallen asleep for a couple of hours. I sat upright and grabbed my phone off of the table to check the time. It was 10:30 pm. I turned my head to the right to see Miya writing something in her notebook on her bed using the lamp as light.

"Miya?"

She closed her notebook and put it back in her bag, "Hey, Owari. You're finally up."

"Did you just wake up too?"

"Nah…I didn't really go to sleep when you did, I wasn't that tired."

"Oh, so what have you been doing this whole time?" I asked, laying myself back down.

"Well I've been writing for the past twenty minutes or so, and my mom called earlier. She was asking where I was, so I explained."

"Was she mad?"

"Not really, she trusts me."

I got up slowly. "I'm glad to hear that."

"I've just been on my phone for the rest of the time I guess, doing nothing."

"Sorry we didn't get to go to the onsen tonight," I said, walking towards my bed and laying on it.

"It's okay, we have tomorrow to do it. I'm not sure why I was so eager to do it earlier."

"Haha it's okay, I liked your eagerness. I would've gone with you tonight if I didn't fall asleep. Wait, did you just want to go now?"

"Isn't it too late now? - like if we went, would we get in trouble or anything?"

"The public ones close at 10:00 pm, but the private ones don't close as long as we don't make any noise."

"Oh really? Well...I think I'm the one who's too tired to do it now, but as I said earlier, we'll do it tomorrow."

"If I fall asleep tomorrow, wake me up!"

"I will~ But oh! Tomorrow's the only full day we have here, so make sure not to fall asleep in the first place."

"That's right! We have to go back on Friday morning to be there in time for graduation. A vacation from Wednesday to Friday seems like such a long time, but I guess it was really only till Thursday."

"...Right..." Miya yawned.

"You going to sleep?"

"M-hm." she pulled the blankets over her and nuzzled into her pillow.

"Goodnight Miya."

CLNK CLNK CLNK

"Huh? What's going on?" I woke up in my bed, Miya still sleeping in the other one. I looked around the room to find waiters bringing in breakfast, again without knocking. I quickly got myself together and walked a couple of steps to the other bed to wake Miya up.

"Miya! Miya!" I yelled to her in a whisper.

She slowly opened her eyes and looked at me. "Good morning Owari. How'd you sleep?"

"Hey Miya, good morning. I-"

"Good morning ma'am!!" a waiter shouted as he was swiftly moving in and out of the room.

Miya jolted up. "Who was that??"

"That's...why I woke you up. They, uhm, came in

unannounced again."

Her face returned to the blank and tired state you'd expect when someone wakes up. "Is this normal?"

"I guess it is…"

Before Miya even got up, all of them had already left the room and put down everything for the first course. Eventually, though, she got up and sat down at her seat across from me at the low set table. She had the slightest smile on her face and was squinting her eyes, still adjusting to being awake. Again, we stuffed ourselves for breakfast. About an hour later, we had finished our meal and started to get ready for the day.

"Hey, what should I wear when we go out?"

Apparently, when I was sleeping, she hung up all the clothes she brought in the closet to not get wrinkled.

"Hm, well it's really nice out today, so you aren't too restricted like you were yesterday."

"I'll keep that in mind~"

"I need to get dressed to go out too, so I'm going to close the sliding door between us to have a little more privacy."

"Kk. Oh! And the windows too. At least fold up the blinds a little bit."

"You're right!"

While I was getting dressed fairly quickly into my usual attire, it took a while for Miya to finish getting dressed. I assume she was trying on multiple different things to see what looked the best. "Hey, sorry I took so long. I think I'm ready now though," she said through the screen door after a couple of minutes.

"Oh, no worries."

I could see the light changing on the other side of the room through the sliding door, so I assumed she opened up the blinds. I did the same to my side.

"Ready?"

"Yep."

I could hear her walking to the sliding door. "I'm going to count down from three and then open the door, okay?"

I made an audible sigh like I was preparing to embark on a mission. With the amount of buildup she was giving me, it had to be better than yesterday's, which seemed almost impossible to me.

"Three...two..."

She opened the door and had this huge smile on her face as she started blushing. Time almost seemed to stop as she opened it. "So? How does it look?"

It looked…amazing. It was hard to compare it to the one from yesterday since it was a completely different style, but this style fits another side of her just as much as the other one did. She had on a fitted plaid skirt that was cream in color with black and white intersecting stripes, with narrow red accent stripes also moving across it. On the bottom, there was also a slit in the front that looked like someone had purposefully cut with scissors. Paired with that, she had a fitted black long sleeve crop top with white buttons on it. She had on a sheen black headband and put her hair into a half-up ponytail and transformed her straight bangs into just two long bangs on the side of her face. On the makeup side of things, she went with a Korean-inspired style full of sparkles. She did a white-winged eyeliner with sparkly reddish-pink eyeshadow and glossed her lips.

"So…you're not going to believe me…but I think you look beautiful, but that goes without saying."

I don't know how, but her huge smile became bigger than before. "Maybe, but since it's me, you have to say it," she said just before making her same impish laugh, walking back to the closet.

"Hm? There's more?"

"Just the shoes, I didn't want to wear them in the room." She bent down and put her head into the closet to reach in the back, bringing back out a pair of ankle boots with the same cream color as her skirt. She held it up slightly to show it to me.

"Woah it matches your skirt, was that planned?"

"Of course it wass."

I started walking towards the closet. "So that must mean you have another outfit planned for tomorrow, right? Can I see?"

She held her arms out to guard the closet, facing me. "Noo! Not yet. You can see it tomorrow," she said matter of factly. She turned toward the closet and closed it, then strutted towards the door, my eyes following her the whole time, astounded. She got to the door and turned around with a huge smile on her face. "Ready?"

"Y-Yes!" I ran up to the door to catch up to her.

"So, where are we going?" she said as she opened the door and was walking down the hallway, still going pretty fast.

"I'm not that familiar with the area...as ironic as that is since I recommended the place."

"No worries, I can look up some stuff on my phone,"

she responded, pulling out her phone to open her Maps app.

"Let me know what you find."

I glanced over to her phone, and she was scrolling through the Maps app, trying to find someplace we could go for the day.

"Looks like…Hokkaido is all nature. Everything is either a park or a spring," she said while laughing.

"It *is* a pretty rural area…"

"Oh, we could go snowboarding," she said, looking up at me. "It'll be pretty expensive to rent two snowboards for the day, but it'll be fun."

"You've done it before?"

"I haven't…but I'd be open to it. What about you?"

"I haven't been either, but we should do it!"

"Aaaaaaaah! Yay! Oh my god, are you scared at all?"

"Should I be?!"

"I don't know…it'll probably be pretty scary the first couple of times we go. But if we're together it'll be less scary."

"Definitely." I let out a nervous sigh.

"You sound really nervouss. We can go somewhere else if you want."

"No, no! I'm okay. It's just scary to think how fast we

could be going down a really steep mountain…it'll be like we don't have any control at all."

"You don't go on the steep mountains when you first start, you go on little ones to get the hang of it, so we'll start there."

"I had no idea, I honestly thought there was just one slope everyone went down."

"So did I until recently, but I wanted to include a snowboarding section in a book I was writing, so I had to research them a little."

"You wrote a book about snowboarding?!"

"Not about - but it included it."

"You have to show it to me when we're eating lunch or something - it'd be very fitting."

"For sure!"

We walked through the long corridors and finally made it to the main entrance area with the receptionist. As we walked past her she got up from her seat asking if we were checking out.

"No ma'am, we're just going out for the day. Our reservation is until Friday morning."

"Okay. Have a good time out," she bowed then sat back

down, typing away at her computer.

"What's up with people acting so weird around us? First, the driver, and now the receptionist," Miya asked curiously but also a little annoyed.

"Hm? She was acting weird?"

"Yeah. You're usually able to go in and out of a hotel without anyone asking where you're going."

"It might be for the same reason the driver was acting weird; older people don't think that highly of young people."

"But in other countries like the United States, eighteen is considered an adult."

"Well, that's just legally. Older people look down on young people everywhere, regardless of whether they are legally an adult or just a kid. It's the same way younger people look down on older people as well…we often think they're not as capable as others.

"I guess…but it is a little bit annoying, isn't it?"

"It definitely is. But Tokyo is a contemporary area, so the people there will be more open to everyone…if that gives you any solace."

"Mn.."

"Anyways!" I said, pulling out my phone. "Don't act so

down, we're on vacation!"

"Are you calling a taxi?"

"Yep," I said, typing out a number I had found online for local drivers.

Fifteen minutes later, a driver arrived, and we were off to the slopes. When he was driving, I had thought about taking control of the wheel from the back and crashing the car into a tree on the side of the road, but it didn't bother me like before after I thought it all out. "Woah...lol that was weird," I thought to myself. That didn't make me feel instantly better, so I thought it out more: so, if I were to crash the car, Miya and I would get injured, and that's the last thing I'd want... So even if I wanted to hurt the driver, which I don't, I wouldn't crash the car.

I turned to Miya...I was infatuated. It was like she had read my mind and had given me the power to overcome those thoughts. She noticed me looking at her and smiled at me without saying a word.

"Here's your destination. Have fun," the driver said as we arrived at the resort. When we were walking away after saying our goodbyes, he called back to us, "Wait! Did you two need a drive back when you were done? Depending on how late you were planning on staying, I could pick you up and drive you back to the ryokan."

"One moment, sir!" Miya wrapped her arm around mine. "Owari, what time do you think we should head back?"

"Hmm…maybe at seven?"

"Oh yeah, just when it's getting dark."

"All we'll have to do is call the ryokan to cancel the dinner later since we won't be there."

"Okay!~" She turned from me to the driver. "We'll be done here at seven. Does that work for you?"

"It sure does. See you at seven."

Miya waved and smiled as he rolled away into the distance. We turned around from the parking lot where the driver had dropped us off, and we found ourselves staring at a huge mountain covered in white.

"Woah…" we both gasped.

"Um… it probably wasn't the best day for a skirt…or a crop top," she laughed painfully.

"Awww." I laughed too. "Don't worry, we're going to rent snow clothes."

About an hour later, we found ourselves climbing up the ski lift to go to our first slope. Now that we were on the mountain and it was snowing, the wind was loud. On the lift, we were about forty feet off the ground and all we could see below us were black dots moving down the slope in rapid succession. I was getting vertigo from looking down, so I turned to Miya who was next to me. I didn't know if it was from nervousness or coldness, but she was shaking. All I could see was her red face since everything else was covered by puffy snow clothes. I was less nervous than I thought.

"You doing okay Miya?"

"Y-Yeah. I am. Just cold."

When it was our turn to get off the lift, I held out my hand for Miya and we hopped about a foot down to reach the ground. The snow was getting very thick at this point, and we couldn't see but twenty or so feet ahead of us. We were on one of the less steep slopes like Miya had suggested, but it was still very intimidating.

"Do you want to go first?" I asked.

"Would it be possible to go together? I'm scared."

"I don't think you can, it'd be too dangerous to get entangled on accident."

"Mmn.."

"There's no need to worry, I looked it up on the way

here and no one has gotten in any serious accident, not even small children."

"Really? Uhm…" She paused and braced herself to descend. "Okay! I'm going to do it. Wish me luck please!"

"Good luck Miya! I'll be down in a second!"

She put on snow goggles that rested on her head, pulled up the mask that protected her mouth, and got into position on the board just like an attendant told us to when we received them. She stood on the edge of the incline for about twenty seconds, then shifted her leg and was off. I rushed to the edge to see how she was doing… She was going really fast. In about five seconds, her figure vanished into the snow, and I could no longer see her. Since everything was white except for our black jackets, when people vanished from my eyesight, it looked like they had fallen off the edge of the earth. I searched around the edge to find other people also going, and there was a group of kids about ten years old going down the mountain without fear of anything. One went after another, and when each of those children vanished off into the snow, it reminded me of what happened just a couple of days prior. I took a deep breath.

You have to go now, Miya's waiting. You have to stop looking. Nothing changes by looking. Hey, you don't even know if that kid died or not...maybe the trees below cushioned his fall and he survived. Wait...but if he did survive...that would mean I'd go to jail for the rest of my life. Would I? Couldn't I make it seem like an accident? I...I mean, it's not like I had any grudge against him...I don't even know his name. I don't even know his name. I don't even know his name. If I just said that I tried my hardest and couldn't end up picking him up, nothing would happen to me...so it'd be best if he did survive, right? Uh...no. That's wrong.

I was standing so close to the edge that a sudden gust of wind tipped the front part of my board down the incline and the rest of it followed. I was now descending the mountain at a rapid speed, struggling to maintain my balance. Luckily, it was an easy incline, so there were no trees or obstacles in the way, but I was very close to falling multiple times. I tipped and leaned and ducked and held my arms out before finally balancing myself. I had no time to put on my goggles, so the snow was pummeling my face. About two minutes later, I finally reached the bottom and met Miya there. I could tell she was extremely jubilant about what she just accomplished.

"Owari!! That was amaazingg!!" Can we *pleasee* go on it again? But…oh! You should go first this time. I want to see how it looks when you go first. Let's go!"

I stood there without saying anything.

"Hm? Owari?" She looked at my face which was covered in snow and red all over from the cold. "Oh my god! Are you okay? You didn't put your goggles or mask on…"

"I got pushed off from the wind, I wasn't ready to leave yet so I didn't have time."

"It's okay, you're okay…" she said while wiping off my face with her glove. Her breath, which condensed in the air, covered her face in front of me. "You're not being very talkative right now. Is it too cold to speak?"

The truth was, I wasn't okay. But not because it was too cold. Every time that scene gets played in my head, I can no longer concentrate on anything but that. Why did I…

"H-Hey, we can stop for now…" Her disappointed-looking face made me focus again.

"N-No, sorry. I was just in shock a little bit since I had never done anything like that before."

"Was it fun at least?"

"M-hm. And now that I know what to expect, I won't go all silent on you next time."

"Yay! It would've sucked if you didn't like it and I went on everything alone. Just remember to not stand so close to the edge, dummy."

"I'll try!"

She held out her hand and we started walking to the ski lift again. We went on the slope just above the lowest one since we now knew what we were doing.

Ten slopes later and we were done for the day. The resort closes as soon as it gets dark for safety purposes, so we were done by 6:00 pm. Now that it was over, I kind of felt empty. Not because I had so much fun to the point where me not having fun now was saddening, but because I didn't enjoy it at all. The thing was, I know I'd enjoy it if I hadn't had that thought plaguing my mind constantly. The only consolation was Miya being there, and she helped the thoughts go away slightly, but it was always somewhere in the back of my mind. I hope I didn't seem *too* distant today, I would hate that.

We were now at the same parking lot we were dropped off at and back in our regular clothes. Miya pulled out her phone to check the time and then looked up at me. "It's only 6:05. We still have a while before our driver gets back...what do you think we should do until then?"

"Since we canceled the dinner at the ryokan earlier, we need to get something around here. I also want to go get something at another store."

"Okay~ Sounds good. Where to first?"

We finished eating at the restaurant and the food was really good. It was a little bit unhealthier than the traditional food we were served at our ryokan but still enjoyable.

Miya seemed to enjoy it too, I could tell by her jovial mood. "So, what store did you want to go to?"

"Let's, uhm...Okay, please don't think I'm weird but I want to go to a hardware store."

"For our new apartment in Tokyo?! Aaaaah! So exciting! Wait, but the place we were looking at already had appliances built in, what did you want to get there?"

"Just some paint."

"Paint, huh? It might be heavy, but we can manage!"

We walked down for a few minutes in the direction of the resort and stopped at an appliance store. We bought two large pales of black paint and a few big brushes. After we picked those up, we walked just a couple of minutes back to the resort and waited for our driver to arrive. Miya wasn't lying, the paint *was* really heavy. Luckily for us, it was already 6:58, so we didn't have to stay long before the driver picked us up.

We were waiting on the sidewalk of the resort when the driver pulled up and rolled his window down to greet us. "How was your stay at the resort? Oh, and I see you got some...paint?"

"It's uhh..."

"It's for our new apartment we're getting in Tokyo," Miya interjected, putting the buckets on the floor and getting into the car, me following closely behind.

"You're moving to Tokyo?"

"We are, yes," I responded, closing the car door.

"That's ambitious, especially since you two are so young. I hope you enjoy yourselves."

"Thank you, sir."

"Thank you."

Eventually, we made it back to the ryokan and went through a side entrance because we didn't want the staff to think we were going to vandalize our room by spreading black paint everywhere. It was a success, and we made it back to our rooms without being questioned. Once we got into our room, Miya jumped on her bed and closed her eyes.

"Are you tired?" I asked while I stored the paint and brushes under our bed, taking out my bag to grab a few things.

"Not physically tired - but since my adrenaline was pumping all day I am a little bit mentally fatigued. Just need a little break, then I'll be back."

"No worries, take your time. I'm going to go outside for a little bit, I'll be back soon."

"Kk. Don't forget a jacket~"

I don't know how, but somehow she knew I was leaving the room without a jacket. I tried my best to silently tiptoe back over to my bag and take out a jacket without her knowing. Once I got it, I went back over to the door and closed it. As I was walking down the hall to the side entrance, which was only accessible once you had a key, I put on my jacket and headphones and walked my way down a dark street, which was only being slightly illuminated by streetlights. It was still cold, so as I was breathing I had a fog appear before me. I put two fingers up to my lip shaped like a 'V', inhaled some, then exhaled all the fog out. Regardless of how old someone is, I know everyone still does it, so even though I felt like a kid I wasn't embarrassed.

○

He seemed distant today. Something was on his mind that he wasn't telling me about. I understand that he might be anxious about moving, but he should be able to tell me about that, right? I feel like he just coasted through today, and if he were to reflect on what happened, he wouldn't even remember. This wasn't the ideal second day (and last day) of vacation, but I can ask him about this when he comes back. I'll update then. Something just...seems off. I didn't want to say anything to him about it, but we're not allowed to paint our apartment in Tokyo because we wouldn't own it, we're just renting it out. I just...don't understand all that much. Maybe something happened between him and Ayama & Asa? Nothing could've happened in person since we've been together this whole time but...I just don't know. Either way, stuff like this goes as soon as it comes, so there might not be a point to this. I won't let this minor bump distract me from how much fun I had today though! And of course, I won't let it distract me from my main mission, asking Owari to be my boyfriend! ...Wait! That's it! He's just nervous about asking me. Aaaaaaaaah this is amazing! He went on a walk to prepare himself to ask me, that must be it. Disregard everything I said previously. If that was the reason he was distant today, it was 100% worth it.

I put my pen and notebook away and went on my phone to catch up on any news. I scrolled for a little and found something that piqued my interest slightly:

"This Just In: 10-Year-Old Boy Found Dead in City of Hokkaido"

"Hmm..?" I said to myself. I clicked on the article and scrolled down a little and dropped my phone on the bed in horror once I saw it. The boy was found dead in our hometown..? I quickly picked up my phone again and started reading the article:

A ten-year-old boy, now identified as Hajime (???), has been found dead in the mountains of Hokkaido. Professionals say that the boy has been dead for at least two days. Autopsies show that the child died after severe head trauma from falling. Government officials are now being questioned about the situation.

"We deeply apologize to everyone involved. We were

oblivious to the fact that the cliff faces in the area were not guarded by rails, much less cautioned via signs. We will continue to invest our efforts into putting up signs and guard rails, and we will readily compensate the parties involved. We acknowledge that any monetary compensation will not cover the full emotional damages caused by this situation, and we are deeply sorry about that. We pride ourselves on being an extremely safe city, so we will work hard to gain the trust back from you all that we have rightfully lost. Thank you." - City Councilman

Hokkaido Central also has contacted the mother of Hajime, but she has refused to give a statement. Be sure to check back to Hokkaido Central for any further updates.

I wonder if Owari has heard about this...Just because I was curious now, I bookmarked the page to get a notification whenever the story was updated. When I closed the website off my phone, Owari arrived.

"Hey, so, are you ready to go to the onsen Miya?" he said as he hung his jacket up and set his phone down on the nightstand.

"I've been ready!"

To be honest, I wasn't really ready. I was super nervous… but still excited. He then told me he was going to shower and then head down to the onsen, and that I should meet him down there whenever I was ready.

He left his phone on the nightstand and grabbed a towel that was in one of the cupboards, walking into the bathroom which connected to a stairwell that led down to the onsen. The shower turned on and I was left there wondering what to do while waiting.

A few minutes after sitting there doing nothing, I heard Owari's phone vibrating from the nightstand and I instinctively went to go check it. If someone important was calling him, I'd be able to answer and say he wasn't available at the current moment.

I got out of bed and walked to the nightstand where his phone was. Once I turned it over, the vibrating stopped and a notification popped up on the screen saying he missed a call from a number that I didn't recognize. I didn't know what to do now, so I just stared at the screen. About twenty seconds later, another notification popped up saying that the person who just called him left a voicemail. I knew I shouldn't have, but I was curious, so I unlocked his phone using the password he told me earlier.

At one point earlier in the day, he had asked me to check the weather using his phone, so he told me the password to unlock it. It was fairly simple to remember, so I typed away and it opened. I went to his call history, and at this point, it was starting to get uncomfortable for me. It didn't seem right to be snooping through his call history, but all I was going to do was check the voicemail...so I guess it was okay. I tried not to look at the other calls, but I couldn't help but glance down for a second.

While he was on the walk, he dialed 1-1-0...the number of the police. The thing was, he hung up before they had a chance to answer. The call was outgoing for about four seconds before the line ended. I stared blankly at the screen for a while before remembering what I had unlocked it for. I clicked on the voicemail and pressed play.

"*Owari! It's Asa. Look. This is crazy. There was this kid that fell off the cliff face you were laying on earlier this week. The thing is, the news is saying that he died around the same time we were there too. Remember when you said that the screaming noise was coming from a couple of kids playing? I'm worried that when we left, something happened to one of them.*

Surely you've heard about this though, right? It's been inescapable on the news for the past couple of hours. Just...call me back when you hear this. This is crazy. I won't be able to sleep tonight."

The call ended and a prompt followed by asking if I wanted to call back. I thought about it, but just turned off the phone and put it back in its original place.

Hmm... So I guess this is nationwide news... Well, at least prefecture-wide news.

My mind was racing at this point, and I was very quickly processing new information about this story and found myself making baseless assumptions: Owari was there? At the time when he fell? And he said he heard screaming from kids playing? What the hell...this all seems so unreal... What if he heard about the story this morning and has felt guilty all day for being in such close proximity to someone dying? This is horrible...I need to talk to him about this...wait...but I'm not supposed to know he was there. How can I bring this up to him? Uhmm... And wait? He didn't have Asa's contact saved. Why didn't Asa's name pop up in place of the number?

I rushed back to the bed where I had left my phone and tried to find any other information I could on this story. I looked back on the website I had visited before, and many, many others. No one else had any other information on the story, and the child's mother hadn't given any statements to any publication. I don't know why, but I started crying. For some reason, I felt as though because I didn't find out anything extra, something horrible was going to happen. My eyes were glued to my phone, desperate to find something else, when I heard something shutter from outside. I looked up from my phone and wiped the tears from my eyes to see that all the windows had been blocked. I was trapped in here. The police must've known that Owari was there, and by blocking all the windows, we'd have no way to escape. He didn't do anything...please... he's innocent. Why do all good things in my life have to last for such a short amount of time?

The room got darker, and I tried to comfort myself by wrapping my arms around my knees and shuffling back to the edge of the bed. The room that once felt expansive and welcoming became that of imprisonment. "Please... someone help me," I whispered.

"Miya!!"

Hm? Someone was calling my name...from outside? I walked up to the now boarded-up window and put my ear to it, crouching down slightly.

"Miya!! I'm in now, you can come in whenever you're ready!"

"Owari! Can you hear me?"

I got no response. I must not be loud enough.

"Owari?" I said slightly louder. Still, no response. I guess all I can do now is get ready to go in.

○

I took my jacket off as I entered the room and put my things down. "Hey, so, are you ready to go to the onsen Miya?"

She put her phone face down and looked at me. "I've been ready!"

"It wouldn't be customary for both of us to go in at the same time, but are you comfortable with that?"

"Yeah, I am."

"Okay. I'll shower then go in first. You can shower and go in after."

"Okay!" she said as she playfully saluted me. "Oh, but how was your walk?" She put her hand down.

"It was very cold like expected, but I just needed a

breath of fresh air, so I'm good now."

I wasn't expecting her to be comfortable being together. I thought she'd want to go in one at a time because she'd be too embarrassed. I'm saying this like I'm not embarrassed myself, but I definitely am.

Once I finished cleaning myself, I stepped outside and was met with a rush of cool air. It wasn't a horrible feeling though, as the steam from the onsen made the air humid. It was a kind of warm-cold air that I wouldn't be able to describe with words. When I stepped outside, there was a square gray button on the wall with a caption under it stating, "To close outside blinds." Not knowing what that meant, I pressed the button and heard something shifting above me.

To get to the onsen, you have to take a private staircase down, which I assume is located in the back of each luxury room in the ryokan. When going down the staircase, the upper floor, where the rest of your room is, sticks out a couple of feet like a balcony of sorts. This balcony was supported by large cylindrical wooden pillars that seemed to have suffered from humidity damage. Anyways, this shifting noise sounded, and since I was under this 'balcony', I could not see where the noise came from. All I knew is that it was from the jutted-out space above me, so I peered my head over the space, and to my surprise, the blinds had covered the whole outside window. I hadn't even noticed the scrunched-up blinds from the outside before. And since they *were* outside, the people inside would have no way of opening them in any capacity. This was actually very smart. However, I was again confused as to whether this was an old ryokan that adopted new technologies or if this was a new ryokan that adopted a traditional style.

I moved from the button to the onsen and touched the piping hot water with the bottom of my foot and recoiled in pain from the heat. "Owww." Eventually, though, my body got used to the temperature and slowly but surely my chest down was submerged in the water. "Miya!" I called out. "Miya! I'm in now, you can come in whenever you're ready!" I got no response, so I assumed she was showering by now.

About twenty minutes later, I heard the door slightly creak open and out of it a voice whispered to me, "Owari…are you there?"

"Miya? Yeah, of course, I'm still here. Are you okay?"

"I'm okay. Can you just turn around while I get in?"

"Oh, duh. Of course." I turned around and faced the fence that blocked the outside world. "I'm turned around now,

I can't see anything."

I heard the door open further and heard footsteps walking on the cement floor to the water.

"Owww!!" She yelled way louder than I did.

"Miya! Are you okay???" I exclaimed, still turned around.

"It's sooo hot. Oww," she said, back to whispering.

"Oops. I uh…probably should've told you about that. Just get in one step at a time, it takes a while."

"I knew it'd be hot, but not *this* hot. Judging by how hot that was…you might need to be turned around for a while," she timidly said while laughing.

"Oh don't worry, I understand. I won't turn back around until you tell me to."

"Thank you." There were a couple of seconds pause before Miya resumed talking. "So, what happened with the blinds? They kind of just… went down suddenly. I was super scared."

"Aaah! Okay so, look to your left. Do you see a gray button on the wall next to the door?"

"I-I think so…what does it say under it?"

"It's a button to close the blinds. It automatically pulls

them down if you press it so people in the room can't see you when you're in the onsen. And as you probably noticed, they're blinds on the outside so you can't pull them back up from inside. The only way to pull them up and down is from that button right there," I said as I heard water moving slightly from behind me.

"Oh? That's super convenient. How old is this place anyway? Something like that has to have been made in like the last ten years or something."

"I thought the same thing, but I have no idea," I said as I once again heard water moving again from behind me.

"So…um…have you heard about what's been on the news today?"

"No, I haven't. Is it something important?" I heard water moving again slightly.

"Yeah, it is. Reports say that a ten-year-old child fell to his death earlier this week."

"What? Are you kidding?"

"N-No, not at all. Apparently, it's been everywhere today, it's national news. I'm in by the way."

I turned around to see Miya on the opposite side of the onsen with her makeup off and her hair pulled up in a messy bun to not get any of it wet.

"How is it?"

She blushed a little. "Now that my skin got used to the temperature...it feels so nice and relaxing."

"The hot water paired with the cool breeze makes it so much better too. Outdoor onsens only work when it's cold out," I said, putting my hands behind my head and closing my eyes.

"I can imagine, yeah."

"You okay Miya? You don't seem that talkative."

"My mind is kind of stuck on that child...things like that don't happen in Japan very often...much less Hokkaido."

I opened my eyes again but avoided eye contact with her. "Oh, right. Well, if they just found him today, there's probably going to be more updates to it as the story develops. This is our vacation, remember? We should be relaxing. I'll tell you what, after graduation, we can worry about this all we want to."

"I-I understand that, but it's still a horrible accident, it'd be impossible not to think about it. Especially since it happened in our hometown."

And impossible not to think about it, it was. I had

thought about it so much today that I almost turned myself in to the police, and that was *before* I knew it made national news. Now we were both worried about it, albeit in completely opposite ways. She said that it was a 'horrible accident' though, so it looks like I'm safe from any suspicion at this point...that's good. What am I saying? Am I only worried about that situation because I'm afraid of getting caught, or because I took a human life? What the hell is wrong with me? I feel like I'm never going to get over this...and it's not like I can tell anyone about it... I'll go to prison for the rest of my life. Did I ruin my life over one *stupid* mistake? I did it for the purpose to avoid judgment from others...and now I'm the one judging myself. I sank into the water and only my head was visible now. I laid the back of my head on the concrete and looked up at the starry sky. The steam was floating through the air and clouding my vision.

"You okay Owari?"

"I'm just...I guess I should tell you that I...

○

"Owari...are you there?" I said as I slightly creaked open the door to the outside.

"Miya? Yeah, of course, I'm still here. Are you okay?"

"I'm okay. Can you just turn around while I get in?"

"Oh, duh. Of course. I'm turned around now; I can't see anything."

I opened the door further and poked my head out to see if he was really turned around. Not that I didn't trust him, I was just being extremely cautious. This might've been different if we were dating, but since we were still just friends it was awkward for me. Either way, now that I was down here instead of looking at it from above, I could really feel and take in the atmosphere they were going for. There were large rocks that surrounded the water, as well as a couple of small trees and other greenery that made it feel all the more natural. In the corner of the hot spring, there was a wooden valve that was flowing water out from it. I dipped my foot without thinking but just as quickly pulled it out and winced in pain. My tiny movement was enough to imbalance the delicate water that was filled to the brim, so it overflowed and spilled out onto the concrete floor.

"Miya! Are you okay??"

Owari showing so much concern in his voice while still

being turned around was kind of funny to me, so it diffused any pain I had. "It's sooo hot. Oww."

"Oops. I uh...probably should've told you about that. Just get in one step at a time, it takes a while."

"I knew it'd be hot, but not *this* hot. Judging by how hot that was...you might need to be turned around for a while," I said, slightly nervous.

"Oh don't worry, I understand. I won't turn back around until you tell me to."

"Thank you."

I tried to dip my foot back into the water, and although it was still painful, it was less painful than before, so I took the plunge and fully submerged it. I was inch by inch lowering my body into the water when I asked about the blinds closing. He explained that it was simply a button he pressed for privacy reasons, and I felt stupid for thinking it was some kind of police invasion. Next, though, I wanted to talk about if he heard the news this morning as I had speculated he had. I was fully submerged from my chest down at this point, but him being turned around helped me talk about something so emotional to me. I don't know why, but it's easier to explain things to people when you can't see their faces.

"So...um...have you heard about what's been on the news today?"

"No, I haven't. Is it something important?"

"Yeah, it is. Reports say that a ten-year-old child fell to his death earlier this week."

"What? Are you kidding?"

"N-No, not at all. Apparently, it's been everywhere today, it's national news. I'm in by the way." Although I had been in for a while now, the hard part was over, so I was comfortable enough for him to turn around.

While we were talking I was looking directly at the back of his head, but when he turned around I darted my eyes away and started blushing. Nothing was showing, but it was still a little embarrassing for me. We talked a little more about the news, and Owari eventually slumped the back of his head on the side of the onsen and looked up to the sky, closing his eyes. He didn't seem okay. Maybe I shouldn't have brought it up.

"You okay, Owari?"

"I'm just...I guess I should tell you that I...I'm just really sensitive about that type of thing, you know? Since my father is so sick, the idea of death, especially death that's so close to me in a lot of ways… is uncomfortable for me."

"I'm sorry for talking about it then. I know your dad is sick and everything."

"You should only be sorry if you did something wrong, and you didn't. I'm sure Asa or someone else would've told me about it tomorrow anyway. It's better you did it now so that I don't get all sentimental in front of everyone."

"Okay. So how does the water feel for you?"

"It feels really good, I feel like my muscles were all sore and cramped from being in the cold all day, so right now everything feels so loose, you know?"

"I feel the same way right n__," I said as I slumped down into the water. Now only the top part of my face was visible.

"Hmn?" Owari said as he opened one of his eyes and looked slightly down at me. He laughed a little. "You look so weird right now."

I laughed too, only no one could hear it and a bunch of bubbles appeared in my face. I shot back up to where I was before and smiled. "I loved this vacation. I don't want to go back to school tomorrow."

"I know right? I feel like we got so much closer too. It

doesn't seem like we're just old friends reconnecting anymore, it feels like we're just friends again."

"Yeah...friends again," I whispered under my breath and looked down a little.

"Oh! And it's graduation day, so it's not like we have any work to d-"

I looked up again, wondering why he cut-off mid-sentence, to see Owari's eyes widened looking directly at me. "Miya...we forgot to do the work I need to do to graduate."

"What time is it...?"

"It's due in two hours."

Chapter 3A

Chapter 3A:
Preparation

God does not exist. Well, God does exist. However, it is a fake God. God is simply a tool made by humans to justify their actions and to be comfortable with death. What happens when you die? Do you get reincarnated? Do you go to heaven? Sounds okay to me. People often say, "No one knows what it's like when you die, and no one will ever know," but I know. I know what happens after death. Nothing. It is simply like before you were born, nothingness. People do not have a soul; humans are simply intelligent beings with way too much self-importance. The ego you must have as a species to think that you have a soul and that the soul can be transferred across generations is laughable. We are nothing. We are nothing but intelligent skin suits that walk around like we're not. Now, does this ideology mean that I do not have morals? Of course not. It's only that I don't get my morals from someone I've never seen. I get my morals from what *I* believe to be justice. This idea is called humanism. No matter the label, is my sense of justice correct? No. But no person's sense of justice is. Not because one is objectively right or objectively wrong, but because there is no way to discern which is. It's interesting to think about how if something cannot be discerned, it cannot be right or wrong.

The idea of heaven and hell, and the thought that people believe in it is illogical in every sense of the word. The concept of hell is just to stop people from doing "bad" things, and the idea of heaven is simply to promote goodness. I mention this because the "bad" things you do now will have no consequences in the eternal void that is death, so would there be a reason not to do them while you're still alive? Life is not eternal, so there is no such thing as an eternal consequence.

Sometimes I wonder if every religious buff is just in on

one big joke. As a child reading a fable, you believe the fable to be true; you have very little understanding of what is fiction and what is not. Religion is the adult version of these fables. This is fine, but the only difference is that religion is treated as law, is treated as fact, and has gotten many people killed. Like I posed before, do people only follow these principles and *pretend* to believe these things to lead a better life, or have they been brainwashed? Am I crazy for thinking this, or does everyone feel this way but not say so because it's socially adverse? I don't want to convert anyone; I just want to understand.

○

It was already 10:00 pm and we only had two hours to do my work. We quickly got out of the onsen one at a time and went into our room. Pulling out my computer, we made it to the teacher's website and started taking all the tests I needed to pass.

"Miya! Originally we had planned to work together to take the tests, but we don't have time for that anymore. I need you to sign in as me on your computer and take a different test than I am at the same time."

"Whatt? But I'm not good at taking tests."

"Whatever you get will always be way better than not submitting it at all. We have to try; I need to graduate."

"O-kay! I'll try my best."

I was busy taking a reading comprehension test, while in the corner of my eye Miya was taking out her laptop and was being tested on geography. "Wait - you're probably better at reading comprehension than I am, let's switch computers."

"Got it."

Twenty minutes passed and we had finished the first two tests, both getting a 100% score on them. We only had one hour and forty minutes left; we needed to move at a much faster pace to do this.

"We won't have enough time Owari. This is an insane amount of work."

"Most people don't do a year's worth of work in two hours, but it's okay. All we can do is try our best. Just try and hurry."

We cut our pace to about twelve minutes per test, every time scoring pretty high for barely taking our time with it. We now had just under an hour left. However, we were still not on pace to even get a 50% for my overall final grade. I wasn't sure what to do, so I grabbed my phone and called Ayama.

Rnng

Rnng

"I hope she's awake…"

Miya turned over to me, confused. "Who're you calling?"

"Ayama. We need all the help we can get."

CLCK

"Ayama! You're still awake! Please, I need your help! Can you log into my school account and take all the math tests for me?"

"What? Take all the math tests for you? Why?"

"I'm taking all of the history-related tests, Miya is taking all of the reading and writing tests, and I need you to take all the math tests!"

"Owari! You're still not explaining why!!"

"I don't have time to explain, please just log in. I'm going to message you my info so you can take them all. Please be quick, you need to finish all ten tests in fifty minutes, okay?"

"What?? Owari wa-"

I hung up the phone and submitted my next test. Now

that I was done with history, it was time to move on to science. Rushing to open the next test, I quickly glanced over to Miya whose eyes were glued to the screen. "How're you doing so far, Miya?"

"Reading tests take a little while longer to complete than others, but I'm getting there."

"Please be quick!"

"Got it!~"

Fifty minutes passed and it was 11:59. My wrists hurt so much from clicking, and my short two-hour burst of energy quickly deflated into the most tired I'd been in a long time.

"W-We did it, Miya," I said weakly, laying down on my back.

"Yeah. We did," she said, laying on hers.

I turned my head over to Miya, who was a few feet away from me on her bed… she was asleep. That has to be the fastest someone has ever fallen asleep. I took out my phone from my pocket and saw that my final grade had been updated to 70% for the year. Looks like Ayama did every single test...wow...that's amazing. I was fading in and out of consciousness, fighting to not fall asleep, but I wanted to thank

Ayama over a text... Even though I was extremely tired, this felt rewarding. I had accomplished something...and I did it with the help of people close to me. This was a great way to finish our vacat...n...

The alarm I had set for 7:00 am on Friday had sounded, so I reluctantly reached over to the nightstand but was stopped when I turned my head over to look. To my surprise, Miya was asleep right there next to me.

My face turned red, and I slightly backed up to get to the edge of the bed without falling off. I tapped on Miya's shoulder to wake her up. "Miya?" I said in a slightly higher-pitched tone of voice.

After I tapped her shoulder, she slowly opened her eyes and started to smile once she got her bearings. "Hey, good morning," she said, sitting up and grabbing her phone.

"Did you sleep okay?"

"I did - thank you. Did you?"

"Yeah...I did." My tone was slightly confused, so she looked at me wondering why that could've been. After a few seconds, she realized, and her eyes widened.

"I slept here last night?"

"A-Apparently." I let out a nervous laugh.

"I don't even remember doing that." She swiftly got up and walked over to the closet to get dressed, embarrassed. "I must've been so tired that I didn't even think about it. I'm sorry, I hope that wasn't uncomfortable for you."

"I didn't even notice you were there until I woke up, and I woke you up as soon as I did, so it's okay. Even if I did wake up to you coming over, I would have been okay with it, so you're completely fine. We're close again like we used to be, remember? Don't worry about it." I walked over to the screen door while she was still taking out clothes from the closet and rested my hands on the side of the door. "Do you want me to close this while you get ready?"

"Yes please."

She didn't look at me when she said this, she still must've been embarrassed. I didn't mind though, I thought it was cute.

Twenty minutes went by and Miya was still getting ready. I didn't want her to feel rushed, so I didn't say anything.

Without warning, a flock of men paraded into the room one after another in chic all-black clothing carrying bowls of food carried on huge trays. They didn't knock or greet me, they simply marched past the two beds and headed right for the screen door where the low table is.

"Wait!" I ran up to the screen door and spread my arms across it. "You can't go in there right now! Please leave the food on the bed!"

"Eh?" all of them said in tandem. Their once jolly faces turned into nasty scowls and they stared at me intensely.

"Please."

They still said nothing. For about twenty seconds, I was having a staring showdown with the man in the front. His eyes would not leave mine. I was dying from the awkwardness. I looked to the side for a moment but looked back to the man to see if he was still staring after a couple of seconds, and sure enough, he was, and so were the other seven men.

"Umm...so are you going to leave it on the bed?"

They stood there in silence.

Out of nowhere, the door behind me opened and there was Miya, headphones in, looking at her phone. Since she wasn't paying attention, she bumped into my arm which was still laid out across the door.

"Huh?"

I turned back to her and she looked up to see what was

in her way. Now, all eight men were staring at her through the door, still scowling.

"Aah! E-Excuse me. What's going on?" she let out as she pulled her phone away from in front of her and onto her right shoulder.

Now that the door was open, the men went back to their happy expression, took their gaze off of us, and marched through the door to put the food on the table. Miya and I stood there in shock, even after they left the room.

"I-"

"Um. Owari, what was that?"

"I'll...tell you while we eat."

I wasn't sure what the eight men were going to do next, so I never took my eyes off of them while they were serving us. Now that they were gone though, I got to look at Miya for the first time after she got ready. She was...wearing gray sweatpants, an oversized pink t-shirt, and fuzzy pink socks? That didn't seem like an outfit she'd wear on her graduation day. She noticed that I was looking at what she was wearing with confusion, but she still spun around like she usually did and asked me how I liked it.

"How is it?"

"You're wearing this on graduation day? Wait. That came out wrong. It's not bad it's just-"

"We have to wear our uniforms on graduation day. Part of the reason I took longer than normal was because I got everything ready for another outfit but realized it would've been useless if I had to take it off just a couple of hours later. Plus I did my makeup and hair, can't you tell?"

"Woah...they allow you to wear makeup at school? I never really picked up on that."

"Only on graduation day do they allow it. It's the last day of school, what are they going to do?"

The juxtaposition between her stay-at-home outfit and her beautifully done makeup and hair was astonishing...in a good way. She didn't do what she did yesterday, she went for a more traditional and formal makeup look, which fit her just as well. As for her hair, she went back to what she had a couple of days ago, which was fully down and straight bangs across her forehead.

"You seem like you don't like it…"

"I just wasn't expecting it, honestly! I thought you'd go all out for our last day here."

"I have all the time in the world to show you

everything, so why rush it, you know? I just want to be comfortable before we have to wear those uniforms again."

I feel like anything I told her about how she looked at this point would've been useless given my first reaction, but I truly did love it. "I know what you mean." I paused, looking back around the room to see that all our stuff was still everywhere. "Alright, ready to pack up and head out? We need to leave soon since the graduation is at 1:30 pm."

"Right, yes. I'll grab all of my things. After we eat though."

"Of course, how could I forget?"

Chapter 3B

Chapter 3B:
The Conviction
Ceremony

After calling a couple of taxis, we finally found one who agreed to take us home. It was a lot harder than I thought, seeing as how the first taxi driver on our trip here agreed to take us that far. We first stopped by Miya's house to drop off her things and change into her uniform, then went to mine and did the same thing. Even though I didn't really like being at school, or being around all those people, I went in with a positive mindset. I felt so independent, so free…and the great thing about it was that

I wasn't independent - I was with Miya now. We were doing everything *together*, it felt amazing. After putting away my things at the house, we started walking on the path to school. This was going to be the last time for a while I took this route, and honestly, I'm sad to see it go. We often get tired of the same old thing every day, we get tired of a routine, but once that routine is over...we beg to go back to it. I hope the excitement that is Tokyo won't ever fade.

After walking for a while, we got to the school.

"It's only noon. There's still about ninety minutes until everyone else gets here..."

"I know, but I kind of wanted to do something first."

"Hm? At school?"

"Yeah. One last time," I said, plopping the heavy bag I was carrying onto the ground to rest my shoulders.

"Does it have something to do with that bag?"

"Mayybe."

"C'mon! You said you'd tell me what was in it when we got here. I can't wait anymore! I'm gonna open it!"

She was expecting me to tell her no, so as she reached down she hesitated a little. When I didn't do anything, however, she made the full motion, unzipping the bag to find the two big buckets of paint. "Wha-? The paint?"

"Yeah, the paint."

"What do you plan on doing with it?"

"You'll see," I said, picking up the bag again after my shoulder rested and heading into the building. Miya quickly followed behind me.

I want to create a message. A message waking up every one of our classmates. This will be the first time I do something *this* drastic to push my viewpoints, but I might as well do it now that it's our last day. There's only one chance for me to do this, so there's no room for hesitation. I might regret this, but I already regret something way worse, so it'll be nothing. I hope Miya is able to help me…I feel like we've grown to be so close in the past week. What better time to tell her how I feel than now? Well…I say all this like my "viewpoint" and "message" are something I think about a lot…but truth be told… they're not. I only think about stuff like that in passing and when it's convenient to me, but I'm tired of that. I'm tired of letting my life pass me by and passively thinking about things I should be doing, things I should be saying, things that I should be pushing myself and others around me to do. My mind is telling me to think about what I'm about to do, think about the ramifications, but my heart is telling me to just do it and worry about what happens later. I started taking control of my life when I asked Miya to go on vacation with me, and as disturbing as it is, I took control of my life when I let go of that child even though I could've picked him up. I was just on the cusp...but now that his body is found...I was pushed over the edge just like he was. All I need to do is tell Miya.

"Where are they going to hold the ceremony again?"

"In the auditorium."

"Got it," I responded, making a sharp left from the main entrance to start heading down the hall. "It's the second door on the right, right?"

"Mhm."

"Okay."

"Owari! You're walking too fast, wait up!" Miya said, rushing a little to catch up to me.

"Sorry, I'm just a little on edge right now."

We made it to the auditorium and a huge room filled with lines of chairs, probably in preparation for the ceremony, were laid out in front of a huge stage-like structure that was slightly raised above the ground from the rest of the room. On this stage, there were massive white curtains that were folded on either side with a small podium on the center stage.

"This is kind of eerie, isn't it Miya?"

"The room has nothing in it...so much to the point where even us basically whispering has an echo."

"I know, weird." I walked up to the stage and climbed on the raised stage platform, hoisting the bag up with me. "Need help?"

"N-No," she said while climbing up. "I got it."

"Okay," I said, walking over to the curtain on the left side.

Miya got herself up and walked over to the curtain as well, putting her hands behind her back. "Sooo. What are you doing?"

"Nothing really," I replied, using a rope to lower the curtain.

"Mmmmm."

I could tell Miya was getting slightly annoyed by how much I was avoiding the questions she was asking, so I finally went ahead and gave in. "This is our last day here, we might as well make our mark, right?"

"Right. So what does that have to do with black paint and curtains?"

"You really don't know?"

I think she had an idea but didn't want to believe it to be true.

"N-No. Not really."

The left curtain was now fully laid out on the floor. It was so massive that it covered almost the entire left side of the stage. Now that it was laid out, I carefully took off the cover to the black paint and picked out the biggest brush in my bag.

"We're going to make a statement. A statement that all people in the school should know about."

"A statement?" she asked, walking closer.

"Yes. To be honest with you, I've been dealing with a lot of negative emotions lately. For some reason, I've been stuck on the fact that people are so disposable, so useless, so fake."

"What do you mean by that?"

This was my time. I had to speak everything I wanted

to clearly and logically to help her understand.

"Ninety-nine percent of the people in this room will go on to lead nothing but disposable lives. Tirelessly laboring day and night to make barely enough money to live. Ninety-nine percent of the people in this room will never talk to each other again, despite how close they feel they are. In this day and age, relationships are not valued at all, people don't care about others as much as we'd like to believe. Two people might call each other best friends now, but when they leave this room their friendship will dissolve almost instantly. Isn't this sad to you? Isn't it sad that most people in this room will go on to lead boring lives and accomplish almost nothing impactful? Isn't it? I just wonder why people are so complacent. Why are people so fake not only to other people...but to themselves?"

"There are...a lot of reasons. For one, someone *has* to take the boring jobs. People like those run society, and people who *don't* do that are the outliers. But I understand where you're coming from. Why bring this up so suddenly though?"

I was caught off-guard slightly by her reply but continued. "To be honest...it mainly stemmed from hearing about that kid who died yesterday. It puts things into perspective for me. He was only ten... In the last moments of his life, he was probably thinking that it ended way too early. This is what's going to happen with everyone here too. I do care about the people in this room though, I care about giving meaning to their lives, so I must remind them...with this...to never be complacent, never say that it's enough. I want people to yearn for more, and above all else, be honest when they do."

I picked up the bucket and started to walk to the top left corner of the curtain, Miya following close behind.

"That makes a lot of sense... Now that you put it like that it *is* sad... But um, didn't you buy the paint before I told you about the kid dying?" And why *are* you so passionate about everyone else...? You don't really know most of them, do you?"

"I originally did want this paint for our apartment, but I remembered that we couldn't use it since we're just renting...and I didn't want it all to go to waste. And I guess I care about everyone else because I'm selfish. I want the world to be a better place so *I* can have a better life."

The truth is that I had this planned from the moment I got the paint, but I couldn't tell her that. Not yet anyway.

"You want the world to be a better place to lead a better life? Isn't that the opposite of selfish?"

"I mean, if people were more creative…outgoing… honest with each other…then we'd accomplish a lot more. We'd put down our pride, be free to express ourselves, and prosper as a species. It would be another renaissance period of sorts. And…I guess that it *is* kinda selfish to want that, at least in the way I want it…because when I think about what would happen during this 'renaissance'…I'm only really thinking about my circle, not anyone else's."

"Oh…well…people aren't built to think globally, it's normal to only think about what would affect you directly. You shouldn't see that as selfish."

"You're right." I paused for a moment, looking down at the ground to avoid eye contact with her. "I know what I've been saying sounds cliché, but will you please assist me in this?"

"Assist you with this? You mean like…help you paint? I still don't know what you're planning."

"I plan to write something like… 'TAKE OFF YOUR MASK' in bold letters with a theater-type mask in the middle.

She tilted her head in confusion. "What do you mean

by writing? Like, on the curtains?"

"I don't really have the courage to get up in front of everyone and tell them how I've been feeling...how I want everyone to be passionate about their future...so I figured the next best thing would be to write it on here...so everyone will see it. On top of that, no one will know it was me who did it."

She started laughing but tried to cover it up with her hands. "You know, that seems a little *too* cliché, even for you."

"I know," I chuckled, "I know. But I can't exactly write a like...whole manifesto on the curtains explaining all of my viewpoints. This will grab people's attention and it will stick with them for a long time."

"I'm still a little hesitant...I've never done anything like this before. I've never even thought about doing something similar...but after hearing what you think, I suppose it's coming from a good place, yeah?"

"I think so, anyway. Plus, there aren't any cameras in here, so we can't get caught as long as we do it quickly. There's no need to worry about any consequences."

"Okay. But if I get too uncomfortable, I'm just going to watch."

"That's fine with me, I'll do whatever makes you

comfortable."

"And before you start...can you promise me one more thing?"

"Of course, what is it?"

"If I tell you to stop, will you?" She took her hands from in front of her and moved them behind her.

"If you tell me to stop, I will stop. I promise you that."

"Okay! Then what do we do first...? Wait...thinking about it more, it's kind of cool and mysterious...it's like right out of a mystery novel."

"It does kind of seem like it's straight out of a mystery novel...it's all cryptic and everything. Only *we're* the ones who know the mystery, and everyone else has to solve it. It's kind of fun being on this side once in a while, right?"

"Right! And maybe I could even write a short story on this! Like...a mysterious man goes into the school and pulls down the drapes to reveal his message! Just then, all the doors lock in the auditorium automatically! And the man says, 'You must take off your masks, if you do not, then you shall perish!'"

"I feel like that's the plot of so many survival game stories. But with your writing style, I'm sure you could make it work. It sucks that you can't write about it due to copyright infringement though."

"Copyright? How?"

"We're about to do your story in real life, aren't we?"

She laughed. "You're being cliché again! Anyways, push me in the direction I need to be in."

"I'll put the paint onto the left curtain. While I'm doing that, please pull the other curtain down. And you know what, I'm not going to use a brush…I'll just dump it.

"Okay."

I started pumping the black paint out of the bucket and it was oozing onto the thick white curtain. I started spelling out the words "TAKE" and "OFF" in a huge print. The letters were so massive that I had to move quite a bit to write out each one. This was so satisfying. Something about destroying this pure white curtain made me feel so…good. A feeling of great excitement rose through my chest and onto my face, which plastered a huge smile across it. Now that I was getting into the groove of it, I started rapidly writing the letters and almost running across the curtain as I did so. The bucket was so heavy, so it felt like it was my mission to relieve the weight from it and put it all on the curtains. I finished the two words and moved on to making the left part of the huge mask when I heard Miya making a noise with the rope. She managed to get it down and laid the curtain out next to the left one.

"If you could, grab a bucket and start pouring the words 'YOUR MASK' onto the canvas - preferably to the side - so I can do the mask in the middle."

"Got it~"

I wonder how Miya was feeling now that she was pouring the paint. Hopefully I didn't make too bad of an impression when I spoke my mind, and I hope she wasn't just agreeing with me to avoid conflict; that'd probably be the worst outcome. Even if she doesn't agree...this is the real me, so... I guess I...never mind, I don't like ultimatums.

In the corner of my eye, I saw her pouring out the letters slowly and methodically, almost to the point where they looked uniform. I was now done with the left side of the mask, so I rushed over to the right curtain and started pouring out the paint to match the mask's other side. Since I moved, Miya noticed me and took notes of how messy and almost horrific the letters and mask looked. After she poured out the first few letters, she rushed back over to the first one and splattered paint all over it, ruining the once uniform word.

"You know what, this is fun." She started pouring out more paint faster than before.

"Exactly. This is a form of expression just like your writing. It'd be silly not to treat this as the same, don't you think?"

"Yeah...this is great." She ramped up her pace and started pouring faster. The paint made a glug sound as it was oozing onto the curtain, and I could tell Miya was getting the hang of it as the bucket became lighter.

Pfft, I heard from somewhere. "Huh?" I said out loud as I looked over to Miya who was now laughing. She had finished the word 'YOUR' and was moving on to 'MASK.' Now that she was embracing my newfound form of expression, I made myself more comfortable and started laughing along with her. This is the best possible outcome I could've hoped for...I felt elated. "Miya! Help me with the mask when you're done please."

She finished with 'MASK' and started moving to the center where I had finished a portion of the mask. We took turns splashing the black paint onto the canvas almost dancing around it like we were in a ballroom. I lifted my hand while pouring and sped up a little, and Miya lifted her hand, sped up a little, and picked up where I left off. Eventually, we met paths during our dance and landed in the middle of the mask. We were both facing each other and had the same idea in that we poured the paint around us, almost encasing our bodies into a small circle. Still laughing, Miya lay down in the circle which was just big enough for the paint to not touch her, and I lay down right there next to her. I turned to her and she was still laughing, now with water welling up in her eyes.

"Ahaaa. This felt amazing. I'm sad all the paint has run out now."

I turned to her, also still laughing. "I know....I couldn't have asked for a better graduation day."

She turned to me and stopped laughing but had the most loving smile.

"Miya.."

"Yes, Owari?"

"Can I tell you something important?"

"Yeah, of course. With all your talk about masking your feelings, it'd seem wrong not to tell me now."

"It would be pretty hypocritical of me, right?"

She giggled a little. "Yeah, it would." She paused for a second while still smiling at me. "So, what did you want to tell me?"

"Well, now that I've told you such an important part about me...I'm now comfortable enough to tell you that I want you to be my girlfriend."

She said yes without hesitation and moved her head forward to kiss me while moving her hand onto my face. "I've been waiting for you to say that you know."

This was the best day ever.

○

Well, this was completely unexpected. When Owari brought out the paint and started putting the curtain on the floor, I had a feeling about what was coming but I didn't think he'd actually do it. This all just...came out of nowhere. Did the story of the child really affect him this much? I had no idea he was capable of something like this...I'm unsure of how to feel right now. I'm trying to push back on what he's saying a little, but the more he explains, the more I find myself agreeing with him. I was confused and concerned when he started opening up to me about how he felt about people being useless, fake, and whatever else. I'm certain he wasn't including me in that generalization, but the thought lingered that he was.

When he told me to paint some, I hesitated but figured I should at least try to lean into it a little…maybe just pour a little…and if I was too uncomfortable, to just stop and tell him how I truly felt. I'm not one to do something I don't like. If I'm uncomfortable, I would say that, and he'd have to honor that if that's how I felt. But…painting it felt so good. To be honest, it was the one thing I'd done in my life that I felt was 'bad' and would have actively destroyed the perfect image the outside world had of me. But Owari was going to be the only one to know about it, so it made me feel amazing. No longer would I have to be ingenuine. Plus, something like this doesn't really matter, right? It's just high school graduation. If painting a few words on a curtain made me more self-confident, even if it's just a little, it's worth it.

As I was painting more, what felt like a thousand pounds lifted off my chest, and the suffocating feeling I was so used to vanished and I was able to think more clearly and breathe more fluidly. This must've triggered some type of chemical in my body because I felt this rush of happiness flow through me, a rush that decided all my actions for me. It felt as though I was moving on my own. I wanted to write now. I needed to put this positive energy into writing something, into my *own* self-expression. I can't believe Owari and I doing something like this would have brought this out of me. This is so uncharacteristic of me. But...I guess humans aren't characters, right? We don't have an archetype. We're free to do whatever we want. So nothing is uncharacteristic for me, or anyone else. Nothing is uncharacteristic of Owari. Nothing is unexpected. This was in him the whole time, and it was in me. I was *just* painting now, but this was more than just painting. This gave me the motivation and energy to write, and write, and write, and I was more aware of my feelings now than I ever had been before. My body moved so elegantly while painting that it almost felt as if I was flying across the curtain, dancing like I was in a performance on stage; the walls spinning around me. But it wasn't just me performing, it was Owari...and this was the part in the story where we crossed paths.

I was tired now, so I lay on my back and Owari also dropped to the floor next to me. I have something to tell you, he says. He says it's important. Is he going to ask me to be his girlfriend? Please be that!

...

"Well, now that I've told you such an important part about me...I'm now comfortable enough to tell you that I want you to be my girlfriend."

"Yes! Yes, I will! Of course, I will!"

Without thinking, I moved forward and kissed him on the lips, putting my hand on his cheek...It was our first kiss. "I've been waiting for you to say that you know."

○

"Okay, we have to get up now to put the curtains back in place."

"'Kay."

We got up and put the top left part of the left curtain on a hook that was connected to a high-tech fly system that automatically put the curtain back in its place. We did the same thing with the other side, let the paint dry, then opened up the curtains to where none of the lettering was showing.

"It's almost time for everyone to get here. We should get rid of these buckets in the disposal bin outside and wait out there till more people arrive." We put the buckets back into the bag and walked out of the auditorium, exiting through a side door where the bins were.

"Come to think of it, why weren't the doors locked?" Miya asked.

"It was honestly just luck I suppose. I didn't know if they'd be locked or not before we came."

"Hmm...so maybe you're not as smart and calculated as you thought."

"Hey! I never said I was smart nor calculated!"

"Huh, really? It sounds like something you'd say."

"I can't believe you think so lowly of me," I responded facetiously.

We dumped the now empty paint buckets into the bin as well as the bag that I was carrying them in. It was already messed up with paint at this point, and we didn't have enough time to go back to my house and drop it off, so we had to get rid of it. We still had about twenty minutes till everyone got here, so we walked around to the indoor greenhouse in the back of the school.

"Woah...I didn't even know there was a greenhouse here! That's so cool! It's hard to believe our school even has a budget for a big indoor one like this."

Walking into the greenhouse, we were met with a wave of warm air and a floral scent. The greenhouse was about the size of a standard classroom, but instead of desks lining the room, it was rows of plants. The gardening club had grown potatoes, soybeans, carrots, as well as flowers like phlox and roses. There were small cement paths in between these rows, but some of the plants grew so big to the point where we had to push them out of the way to move through them.

"It's so cold here year-round that the only choice *is* indoor greenhouses," I said. "And it does seem pretty old...so they probably built it when the school was first made."

Miya walked up to the tall rose patch and smelled one of them, picking it out from the main bush. "Here. For you, Owari," Miya said, using the rose as a microphone before she held it out for me to grab, smiling.

My face got hot and red.

"You're eighteen years old and you're getting flustered by someone offering a rose to you?" I thought, frustrated at myself. Although I was flustered, I couldn't help but smile. "Thank you, Miya," I said, smelling it too.

"You're welcome," she said, turning back around to

continue walking down the row. She kept walking for a couple of seconds before getting to the end of the row when she paused, halting all movement for a couple of seconds. "Our first plant should be a rose!" she exclaimed, turning around quickly.

"I. Love. That. Idea!" I said, catching up to her at the end of the row.

"A rose in Tokyo...Tokyo Rose. That's a good name for a flower shop...what if we made a flower shop??"

"A flower shop called Tokyo Rose? Given the history of that name, I don't think that's the best idea...but that sounds so fun."

"We don't have to make it our main job or anything, just something on the side. A passion project of sorts that just happens to make us money."

"Sounds perfect."

We continued our tour of the greenhouse and Miya was constantly thinking of new ideas for our future flower shop. Not only was she thinking about different plants we could grow, but she was bouncing ideas off me such as new names and an aesthetic we could go for. This sounded fun to me. Not only would we have our own plants on our balcony, but we'd have a whole shop of plants that we could share with others.

"Time to head back now, people should be arriving soon."

"Aww. Okay."

Heading out of the greenhouse, the colder air outside hit us hard, so we speed-walked back to the main entrance. Once there, we were greeted by teachers who were giving out pamphlets about the ceremony. We grabbed them and went to the auditorium to sit in our seats, getting separated by the seating arrangements. The seats were arranged alphabetically, so I was somewhere in the back left while Miya was closer to the front middle. Each seat had a nametag on them, and each row had a letter on the side, so I looked for the 'S' row and went down the aisle until I found Sano. Not all the students were there yet, but some were scattered around the auditorium. Ayama was there a few rows ahead of me.

"Hey! Ayama!" She turned around, confused as to who was speaking to her. Once she saw it was me, her demeanor relaxed.

"Owari? I didn't know you'd be coming today."

"Asa didn't tell you?"

"I guess not...Anyways, do you finally want to explain why I was up till midnight doing your math work?"

"Oh...yeah. Um, sorry about that. But since I didn't do any work over the year, I had to turn it all in on the last day. Thank you so much for that by the way."

"You're welcome. I wasn't really doing much anyway, and I was already on my computer, so it's fine."

"Okay good. Well anyway, it's nice to see you after a couple of days. Do you know where Asa is?"

"It's nice to see you too, I hope your vacation was nice. I haven't talked to Asa today though. I was kind of busy getting ready."

"So he at least told you I went on vacation, huh? Well, I never really told him that...but…"

"Mm. He said you were going somewhere with Miya; didn't really say when you'd be back though."

"Got you. Okay. Well, I'm sure he'll show up eventually, probably late though."

She laughed and turned back around. "Yeah, probably."

BZZ

I pulled out my phone to see what the notification was.

New Message from: *Miya*☆
→ I'm kind of nervous. Is that normal?

I looked to my left to see if Miya was okay and she was simply sitting in her seat looking at her phone. Regardless, I wanted to comfort her, so I responded right away.

Who isn't nervous on their ← graduation day lol?

She responded just as quickly.

→ Not about graduation. I'm nervous because of the message.

The most that'll happen is we'll ← get a few gasps. No one will know it was us. Everything is going to be okay. As long as you don't yell out something like "It was us!!" no one will know. No one is going to psychoanalyze your body language or something.

→ I guess you're right. (· · ;)

I put my phone back in my pocket and looked back up to look around the auditorium. More people had arrived now, and I saw the back of Asa's head in the front row. I was too far away from him to call out, so I just stayed in my seat. Part of me thought Asa would've turned around by now to yell out to either Ayama or me, but I guess even he was nervous today.

I exhaled and looked down, crossing my arms and closing my eyes. I was tired from vacation, and the ceremony wasn't going to start for a couple of minutes. I opened my eyes a few minutes later as I heard music start to play. While my eyes were closed, I could hear shuffling from around me and people talking, but I was sure not more than five minutes had passed. Apparently, that was not the case, and while I was away, the whole auditorium filled up. Even the seats around me were crowded with other students. I kind of felt bad they most likely had to maneuver around me to not bother me. Shaking off my embarrassment, I looked at the stage and important academic figures were seated. The music concluded, and the principal walked up to the podium in the center of the stage to give a speech. The speech was a typical one, one where most of the students weren't even listening and some were even dozing off. However, I was listening intently. Not because I was interested in what the principal had to say, but because I was on the edge of my seat waiting for them to close the curtain.

Next, the student council president walked up to the podium, bowing to the principal as they switched spots, beginning his speech. Afterward, he began calling out names to receive their diplomas.

"Anno, Asa. Please come up to receive your diploma."

Asa stood up awkwardly and quickly as if he were in the military. I couldn't see his facial expression, but he was definitely not his usual Asa self. Although, this was probably because his overenthusiastic parents were on the sidelines taking pictures and crying. He walked up to the side of the stage where there were stairs leading up, which were previously locked for some reason, received his diploma, bowed, then walked back to his seat for the next person to be called. Everyone was called up one at a time, so this was going to take forever.

About twenty minutes later, the council president

called out Miya's name. "Kokoro, Miya. Please come up to receive your diploma."

Miya stood up in her usual methodical manner, hands together in front of her torso, taking strides. She walked up to the staircase, bowed, and politely took the diploma, reaching both her hands out, bowing again, and walking off the stage on the other side. She was probably extremely anxious about being in front of all those people, so I took a big breath as if I were the one walking up there. I was proud she was able to keep her composure.

What felt like two hours passed and it was Ayama's turn to go up. I knew she would be fine; I wasn't worried. I was now preparing myself for my turn to go up. For some reason, I was imagining the curtains somehow closing while I was up there, revealing the message while I was at the forefront of it all. If this happened somehow, it'd be a supposition for anyone to think I was the person who wrote it, but I guess it doesn't matter what logically would happen, anxiety often overpowers it.

"Sano, Owari. Please come up to the stage to receive your diploma."

I took another big breath before standing up. I walked

through my row and made my way to the right side of the stage to walk up the staircase. My heart was beating extremely fast, yet everything seemed to move in slow motion. As I was walking up the stairs, I was looking down at my feet to ground me, but once I moved up passed the stage, I looked up. The stage lights were uncomfortably radiating down, so it was hard to look up at anything past eye level. Regardless, I walked up to the podium and did the normal procedure everyone else had done and walked back to my seat. While moving back to the 'S' row, I looked at Miya who was smiling at me. She looked equally as proud of me as I did of her. This put my mind at ease, and I sat back down in my seat substantially less anxious than I did when I got up.

What felt like hours passed and the rest of the names were called and now all students had received their diplomas.

"Thank you to all teachers, staff members, students, parents, and anyone else who helped the school year be as successful as it was. I hope to continue to build relationships with all of you and I hope you all will enjoy experiencing new things on whichever path you decide." The president stepped to the side of the podium, bowed, and sat back in his seat; the principal taking his place.

"This concludes our graduation ceremony. I hope it was enjoyable for everyone. Thank you for your participation today. Above all else, the level of scholarship we achieved throughout this year was incredible, thank you for studying hard. The school band will play a farewell song, and once that has concluded, students will be dismissed row by row." The principal stepped to the side of the podium, bowed, and sat back in his seat. As he sat back down, the band started the farewell song from behind us and everyone stayed seated in their spot, waiting for it to be finished. I turned my head back to the band, as most students did, but after about five seconds I turned my head back to the stage. While I was turned around, the curtain started to slowly close. I noticed this and immediately poked my head out from the crowd to Miya, who turned back to me with a slightly apprehensive expression on her face.

It was really happening.

The band kept playing their sentimental song, oblivious to the fact that everyone's full attention was now turned to the stage curtains. I widened my eyes as if I was surprised it was there, because, in all honesty, I couldn't believe it was happening. It didn't hit me until now what I had done. Throughout the ceremony, the painting we did on the curtain was in the back of my mind, but it all seemed so unfamiliar to me, like, I couldn't have *really* done something like that. But now that the painting was really in front of me, and everyone was looking at it, it all set in. I could tell people were noticing from the body language in front of me, but I couldn't see what their expressions were, so I turned to the person on my right. I had never seen such a confused, mortified, and scared face before. The student's eyes were unnaturally open, and his jaw was slightly ajar. No one had said anything up to this point. There was complete silence except for the still unaware band.

I tilted my head to look down at the rest of the row and everyone had the exact same expression. No one was even checking to see how each other was reacting, their eyes were all glued to the words on the curtain.

TAKE OFF YOUR MASK

One of the band members must've taken notice, because one instrument after another stopped playing until the whole room was silent. Not a single person was making any noise.

The principal and all other important school figures stepped out of a side door that led backstage to the auditorium. They hadn't noticed what was happening at first, but once they looked at the crowd to see everyone's stunned faces, they all simultaneously turned their head in the direction everyone was looking. Soon enough, all of them had the same face. I think the principal had felt some sort of responsibility for this seeing how he was the head of the school, so he ran back through the door after about thirty seconds of looking at the stage.

"Excuse me, class. I- uh...I'm unsure of why that message was plastered on the board. Fear not, this is not some type of terrorist attack. Everyone will be fine. We will resume our dismissal in an orderly fashion. Please excuse the message, staff are unsure as to who put it there, but we will look into it. Thank you for your cooperation."

After he announced this, the silence broke and people started yelling.

"Terrorist attack?!"

"How does he know? He didn't even know it was there until a couple of seconds ago!"

"Take off your mask? What does that mean?"

"Yeah! For all we know it *is* some type of terrorist message!"

"How can you be sure?"

"Take...off your mask?"

"And what's that symbol in the middle?

"It's a mask, idiot."

"I'm scared!"

"Why else would someone put that there if they didn't intend to harm us? It has to be a sign!"

"Maybe it was a higher power who put it there to warn us!"

"Shut up."

Well, this turned out a lot different than I thought it would. I didn't think people would think of the message as some sort of attack, although it seems clear that something like that would be the outcome in hindsight. Either way, in order to cover up all the chaos that was surely about to ensue, one of the staff members closed the curtains back up to where the whole stage was now visible. The principal walked back out of the door and made sure to keep a calm composure to not worry anyone. People were unnaturally quick to notice his tranquil expression.

"Well...the principal doesn't seem that worried, so I guess it was just a prank from someone."

"Who would do a prank like that?"

"Yeah."

"Now that you mention it, who would want to terrorize a high school graduation in Hokkaido of all places? Stuff like that doesn't happen here."

"But what about the kid who died earlier this week? What if this is related to that incident?"

"That was just a one-off thing."

"Mm...you're right."

Just as quickly as people started to worry, they were all calm again. I didn't realize until now how much value people put on authority figures in tense situations. If the leader is calm, the subordinates will also be calm. Two ends of the extreme played out in a matter of minutes. Either way, I still got my point across successfully; people weren't going to forget this for a while. No matter if they thought it was an attack or prank, the message will seep into people's minds.

'A' was called and Asa, who was in the middle of row 'A', broke out of order and got in front of everyone. I could tell that he was desperate to get out of the school to avoid the embarrassment from his parents. Soon after, Miya, Ayama, and I got up and made our way out of the auditorium. I thought they'd be waiting for me outside the school, but they were both waiting for me outside the doors of the auditorium.

"Miya! Ayama! You both looked great up there."

"You too, Owari. Though I could tell you looked a little nervous," Miya noted.

"Y-You could?"

"Just kidding~ I wouldn't be one to talk anyways." Miya turned to Ayama, who was standing to her left. "Were you nervous Ayama?"

"Not really when I was going up there. But I was scared for a minute when the curtains opened to reveal that weird message. Do you guys have any idea of what that could be about?"

Students were flooding out of the doors and were brushing past us since we were in the way.

"We should probably move from the entrance, yeah?" I responded loudly to compensate for the passing mumbles from the other students.

"Oh, yeah, definitely," Ayama said.

All three of us walked outside the main entrance and to the courtyard where there was a lot more space. There, we met Asa and his family who were still taking pictures of him. He heard me talking to Miya and turned around to us, hoping to escape the spotlight from his mom. "Owari! Ayama!"

"Wait, Asa! We need to take a couple more pictures with the fountain in the background!"

Asa didn't turn back to her and continued talking to us. He put one hand on his hip, the other one straight down holding the diploma. "That ceremony was soo long. I was very, very bored. Well, right up until the end, right Owari?" he said as he wrapped his arm around my neck.

"Well, yeah. I have no idea what that message even meant, much less who put it there."

"Eh? I didn't say anything about who put the message there. I don't really care about that right now. What I care about is the intentions behind the message!" he said as he spread his other arm out and panned it across the sky.

"The intentions behind it? That's awfully inquisitive of you Asa," Ayama added.

Asa stopped for a moment and looked at Miya, who was looking to the ground, probably feeling slightly out of place since she wasn't friends with the two of them. "W-Well, I'm a new person, you see. I am no longer the irresponsible Asa you once knew. As of today, I shall be dubbed Asa the Inquisitive!" he yelled as he pumped his fist in the air.

"Uh-huh. I believe it," Ayama replied.

Asa was joking about that obviously, but Ayama's sarcastic reaction put his spirit down a little bit. He unwrapped his arm around me. "So, Miya...what do you think about what happened?"

Miya took her gaze off of the ground and looked at me for a split second before looking at Asa. "Well, I think it's like something straight out of a mystery novel. I also wonder about the intentions of whoever wrote it."

"See? Very interesting, right?" Asa said as he wrapped one arm around Ayama and one arm around me into a huddle formation. "Anyways," he whispered. He paused for a second then took his head up from the huddle. "You too, Miya!"

Miya looked surprised and apprehensive about it, but

after a couple of seconds, she went into the huddle and wrapped one arm around me and one arm around Ayama.

"Anyways, back to what I was saying, I've heard some people calling what happened 'The Conviction Ceremony'."

"The Conviction Ceremony? What does that mean?" Miya whispered back with a confused look on her face.

"Well, obviously it's about that message from earlier. Conviction refers to the bold message on the curtains, and ceremony refers to the graduation. Hence, 'The Conviction Ceremony'," Asa replied matter of factly.

"I don't mean to burst your bubble Asa, but you haven't spoken to anyone but your parents since we left, and you were the first one to leave the auditorium. You couldn't have heard anyone talking about it," I said as I stared at him with a blank expression.

"Ehm!! Regardless!!" he yelled, obviously embarrassed that he was caught in a lie, "I don't think th-"

KA-CHCK

"Eh?" Asa pulled his head out of the huddle to see his mom taking a picture of us. "Hey! We're in an important meeting," he yelled, breaking the formation we were in.

"I know, I know, but I just love how close you are with

Ayama and Owari," his mother said, dismissing him while smiling. "Oh, and who's this beautiful young lady with you?"

"This is my girlfriend, Miya," I said as Miya bowed to her.

"Nice to meet you, Mrs. Anno."

"And nice to meet you, Miya."

"Huh?? Girlfriend??" Asa butt in as Miya blushed. He took notice of this and continued talking; now embarrassed himself. "Annyyways. We're discussing something very important, mom."

"Is it about The Conviction Ceremony?" she replied enthusiastically.

"Yes, now leave us be for a couple of minutes please."

Are you kidding me!? Was Asa really telling the truth when he said people were calling it that?! Or do he and his mom just share the same brain cell??

"Huddle back up p-lease!"

"Do we have to?" Ayama said, now tired of Asa's antics.

"Uh." Asa crossed his arms in a defensive position. "I guess we don't have to...But anyway, this should be something we look into. Let's go on social media and see if any of our classmates have been exhibiting worrying behavior. We'll make sure to not miss anyone...with this," he said, pulling out the small white pamphlet that he was now holding between his fingers.

This was the most serious I had ever seen Asa; it was quite amusing. He wasn't going to find anything on social media from anyone relating to the situation, but I wanted to egg him on a little, so I let him continue talking.

"If anyone, and I mean ANYONE, seems even a *little* suspicious. Alert me and I will look into it. Got it, everyone?"

"Got it," we all said, some of us more enthusiastic than others.

We turned around to Asa's mom now, who was talking to Asa's dad a couple of feet away from us. Once she noticed we were done talking, she walked back over to us.

"Do you all mind if I take a group picture of everyone? This will be the final one, I promise Asa!"

"Momm!"

"I don't mind," Miya replied.

"Yeah, that'd be fun," Ayama said.

"Sure."

Asa's Mom's eyes lit up and ushered us to the fountain

where we would be taking a picture in front of. Most of the students and their parents left the school at this point, so it was just us in the picture and no one in the background. In order from left to right, it went: Asa, Ayama, me, then Miya. I looked to my left and Asa seemed completely done with the picture taking at this point, so he didn't even attempt a smile. Ayama on the other hand was actually happy to take a picture, so there was a big, genuine smile on her face while she was clutching her wrist to the side with one hand and holding her diploma with the other. I found that Asa being so done with the photo-taking was extremely funny, so when his mom took a picture I had a genuine smile on my face as well.

"Can we see it, Mrs. Anno?"

"Of course, Ayama."

"I want to see it too!" I said.

"Me too," Miya added.

The three of us walked up to Asa's mom who was ten or so feet away from us, but Asa stayed behind at the fountain and looked at his mom with a dumbfounded, blank expression.

"That looks amazing!" Ayama said. "And oh my god, you're so photogenic, Miya."

Miya started blushing. "Thank you."

After Ayama and Miya were done looking at it, Asa's mom turned her phone screen to me. Miya's pose and expression were so…expressive. I don't know what other way to put it. I just…didn't think she would've done something like that in front of people she wasn't that familiar with. She put her right leg behind her in the air and her right hand was doing a peace sign while tilting her head and smiling.

"Woah…this is a really good picture," I said, continuing to look at it.

"It is! And I wouldn't have expected something so animated from you, Miya," Ayama said.

"Well, I…since it is our last day…I wanted to go out of my comfort zone a little bit. What have I got to lose?"

"I agree. It's important to go out of your comfort zone every so often, that way you can make a new, bigger, comfort zone," Ayama replied.

"M-hm."

It was then that I noticed something in the background of the picture. I could just barely see it, but someone was standing behind the fountain holding something, a rose. They were holding it right up to their chest and smiling into the frame. Their face was split in two by the second tier of the three-tiered structure, so I couldn't see their eyes, but the bottom half of their face was visible just enough to recognize who it was.

Hajime, the boy who was reported dead just yesterday, was staring at me through the fountain, holding one of the roses from the greenhouse.

I moved my sight off the phone and to Asa's mom, who was still fawning over the picture, unbeknownst to the deceased child peering at us behind the fountain. I turned back to the picture for a second, but Asa's mom took it away before I could really confirm if what I was seeing was actually there or not. I couldn't see much, but I don't think that I saw any red behind the fountain when she moved it away.

"Do you all want to come back to my place to celebrate?" I suggested to get my mind off things.

"Oh, yeah! That sounds great. I haven't been there in a while."

"Ooh, sure."

I turned back around to Asa. "Yo, Asa. Do you want to come? We're going to my house to celebrate."

"Of course I do!" he said as he ran up to us. "Mom, can

you please hold my diploma while I go to his house?"

"Of course. Have fun!"

"Well, we'll be off then. Thank you for the picture, Mrs. Anno." I waved goodbye.

"No problem Owari. I'll have Asa send it to all of you later."

"Thank you."

"Bye Mrs. Anno."

"It was nice meeting you."

We walked back through the paths to my house, and it was mainly uneventful. Asa was just sharing his theories about what the message on the curtains was supposed to mean, he even coined the term 'Conviction Bandits', who were apparently the ones responsible for the message. Ayama was playing along a little, but Miya was mainly silent. I think she was too nervous to say anything in case she let something slip out, but she was just being overly cautious.

We arrived at my house after about twenty minutes, and I asked everyone to leave their shoes at the door once we got to the entrance. I let everyone step in before me and closed the door once all four of us were in.

"I haven't been here in so long," Ayama said, walking

and looking around, reminiscing on old memories.

"Me either, it's been a while," Asa said, sitting down on the couch and reclining his feet like he lived here.

Miya stayed by the door; she didn't know what to do.

"Oh, by the way, Owari, did you get my call? I left you a voicemail-"

Suddenly, I heard my dad calling out my name from his room. All the lights were off, so before I went to his room I turned on a lamp. I got to the door, and he was on the floor frantically moving around. He was sweating profusely and looked to be in great torment.

"Are you okay?!" I exclaimed, moving into the room and bending down to get to him. I put my hand on his forehead to check his temperature and he was blisteringly hot.

"Everything okay in there, Owari?" Asa yelled out from the couch.

I didn't have time to respond, I had no idea what was going on or what to do. I had never seen it get this bad, would the normal medicine even help him at this point? I...I...

At that moment I realized what had happened. No one was there to give him his medicine all week while I was gone.

This whole time he had been left here with no one to take care of him. How could I be so careless? I let down the one person whose validation I care for the most: my father's. I had never forgotten to give him his medicine before, there had never even been any close calls before this week. I didn't know what was going to happen. All I knew is…he was in a delirious state of mind and couldn't think straight.

"I'm going to get you your medicine, okay? Just lay still." I said, getting up from his room and going to the kitchen.

"Owari…is everything okay? You look worried," Miya said, still standing by the door.

"Excuse me Ayama," I said while pivoting past her to the kitchen. I grabbed the medicine from the cabinet along with some water. "Everything's fine Miya, my dad's just a little unwell right now. It'll be okay."

"Okay…"

I rushed back to the room and bent down again to give him some water. I took out some of the medicine from the container and held it out in the palm of my hand but he refused it.

"No. I don't need it. I'm fine." he said, drinking the water.

"No, you're not. You need to take this. You haven't taken it in a few days."

He pushed my hand back to me and got up from his futon. I stayed there, frozen, while he walked up past me and out of his bedroom door. "We have guests?"

"Hi Mr. Sano, I'm sure you remember me, right? I'm Ayama. And Asa's on the couch over there."

"No. I haven't seen any of you two before. Are you Owari's friends?"

Asa stood up from the couch. "Yes, we are. We just came from school. And over there by the door is Miya."

"Hi, I'm Miya. It's nice to meet you."

"Owari! Who are these people?"

I stayed there, still shocked. He hadn't gotten up from his room in years.

"Owari! Get over here!"

I was shaking now, but I slowly was able to pick myself up and walk to the doorframe of his bedroom.

"Mind telling me who these three are?" he asked commandingly.

"They're...classmates of mine. It's graduation day, so

I figured we could come here and celebrate," I said, looking at the pills in my hand.

"You...graduated today?"

"Yes."

"Oh."

There was an awkward silence in the room for a few moments, so I picked my head up to look at everyone and he was just standing in the middle of the room lifelessly. Arms flat to the side, slightly slouching down; lifeless. Everyone looked at each other and then looked back to him, waiting for him to say something.

"Now that you all are here... It's time I tell you something very important," he said.

"Important how?" Asa responded.

"You see...there's a prophecy. I haven't been able to tell anyone, but I'm sure you all are a bright group, so you may be able to provide some insight on it."

"A prophecy?" Ayama asked.

"Yes. Before I get too carried away, let me lay it all out for you," he said while wiping sweat off his forehead and profusely breathing. "There's a prophecy stating that in the next forty-nine months the world will end. All governments will collapse, all relationships will be destroyed, and most importantly, all human life will cease to exist." He walked forward to the center of the room, facing Asa, who had a worried expression on his face. Ayama was now behind him, I was to the left of him, and Miya was to the right of him. "This prophecy is as old as time itself. So fear not, this is not a fallacy. It is one hundred percent true."

Asa stood still for a moment when suddenly his worried expression transformed into one of laughter. "You actually got me for a second with this whole prophecy thing, that was funny."

My dad's face turned from one of seriousness to one of disgust. "It is TRUE. Do not laugh. How could you laugh at such an important matter?" he shouted as if he were a commanding officer yelling at his recruits. "I would not joke about such things. I do not find this funny in the slightest. Let me repeat myself…all human life will cease to exist. Even you, Aka."

"It's Asa-!"

"And you!" he yelled, cutting off Asa to point at Miya. When he did, Miya jumped slightly and crossed her arms vertically across her chest in a frightened position. He turned around to Ayama and pointed. "And you!" And then me, pointing. "And you, Owari," he said sincerely. "And there's nothing we can do about it," he murmured, crouching down to the floor in a fetal position with a solemn look on his face.

"Dad...it's time to go back to your room," I said, walking up to him and putting my hand on his shoulder.

Almost instantly, he moved his arm to get my hand off his shoulder and stood back up. "Bah! You all don't believe me, do you? I don't have to prove myself; you'll see in forty-nine months! You'll see...and then, while you're on your deathbed, you'll think, 'He was right!'"

Asa dashed away from the front of the couch to where my dad was, pushing him in anger. My dad fell back from his position and was now laying on the floor. "You asshole! It was one thing to spout your nonsense about a dumb prophecy, but it's another thing to say that I'll be laying on my deathbed thinking about whatever the hell you're talking about!" Asa yelled.

My dad got back up, wiping his chin which was now bleeding from hitting it on one of the corners of the cabinet. "As I said, you don't have to believe me. Just wait and see."

Asa walked closer to him and dialed his arm back to

punch him when Ayama stopped his arm mid-punch. "Asa, wait! It's not worth it. No matter how you feel about what he's saying, violence is not the answer to something like this! Especially to Owari's dad."

"Ughh! But he just said we were all going to die! How can you just stand there and take that?" Asa replied, inching forward little by little to my dad while trying to push Ayama out of the way.

I was so engrossed by everything that was happening that I completely forgot about Miya, who was in the corner of the room…crying. I only noticed her because she was actually *audibly* crying. Once I heard, I turned to her, and she was wiping her tears off; makeup melting down her face. I turned back to Ayama, who was still trying to calm down Asa and didn't yet notice Miya was crying. I ran over to Miya to comfort her the best I could.

"Hmph. It's not like all of you will die in exactly forty-nine months. That'd be impossible without the help of some kind of nuclear bomb. Everyone will die *within* forty-nine months. It could be a year from now, a week from now, or even tomorrow. The thing about it is, you won't ever know. You will live the last forty-nine months of your life on the edge, waiting for your last few moments."

"Oh hell no. Ayama, let go of me!" Asa grunted as he tried to shake her off. "He is taking this WAY too far!"

"Asa, wait! He's not in his right mind. Can't you see? He hasn't been medicated in the last couple of days since Owari has been gone. He doesn't know what he's talking about. Don't feed into it!" Ayama shouted as she clutched his arm harder.

"I don't care if he's crazy or not, you have to be held accountable for the things you say! Do you even hear what he's talking about? He said we could die tomorrow! That we'd have to live the rest of our life paranoid because of this! Now. Let...go!" Ayama's grip was cut loose by Asa's other hand, and he started to dial his arm back again for a punch.

My world paused. I could hear Miya crying, Ayama screaming, and saw Asa midway through throwing a punch at my dad. Everything was happening in slow motion, and it was almost as if I was viewing the situation from an omniscient viewpoint somewhere above me.

Is my dad...crazy? I've...never thought of it like that. But in Asa's defense, I didn't even know what to think of what my dad was saying. I mean...it was...crazy, right? There's no way something like that could be true. It's just as Ayama said...I hadn't given him his medicine; he wasn't in his right mind. There's no way I could defend what he was saying or doing.

But...he's my dad.

Something clicked inside me. I ran across the room to Asa and grabbed his arm before he could contact my dad. "Asa. It's true, what he's saying. The world is going to end in forty-nine months. He's not crazy."

Asa stopped. "Owari, what are you saying? How can you be on his side in this? You of all people should've recognized that your dad is just a crazy old man who needs medicine every day just to barely function properly!!"

"He's not crazy! Stop saying that, now."

Logically, I knew the world wasn't going to end in forty-nine months. There was no possible way it could, regardless of if there was a prophecy or not. But I couldn't just stand there and let Asa trample all over my dad's character and tarnish my name. He wasn't crazy. I wasn't the son of someone crazy. I can't let Asa, nor anyone else judge my dad despite everything he's been through. This has gone too far.

"Eh?? Owari, *you* need to think straight! He's crazy! And I'm starting to feel like you are too," he seethed, breaking free of my grasp and moving forward again since my dad had stepped back further to avoid his punches.

Ayama got in front of him again to hold him back, grunting out of effort from Asa's seemingly undying quest to move forward.

"Say he's crazy one more time and I'm kicking you out, Asa."

"Fine... YOU'RE the crazy one Owari. You didn't attend school all year, you suddenly went to a mystery location with Miya, who you haven't spoken to in months mind you, and you've just been acting super weird lately! I bet you're the one who wrote all that shit on the curtains. It has to have been you!"

I ran over to him from Miya and flew my fist to his face. He got knocked down to the ground, yelling out in pain. He was now holding his nose and his face was scrunched up. As he fell, he collided with the couch that made a screeching noise as it moved across the wooden floor. "Leave. Now. You're unwelcome here, Asa."

"Fine! I will leave," he snapped, getting up, still

clutching his nose. "Have a fun graduation party you three. Not that it even matters since the world is going to end in forty-nine months! ...assholes."

I watched him walk to the door, almost pushing Miya out of the way once he reached it, slamming it behind him. I stood there, looking at the door, speechless.

I can't let Asa get away with saying those things. I can't. Asa has to pay for this somehow. Not only for ruining our graduation day, but for calling my dad and I crazy.

My dad is not crazy...he's not. Th-the prophecy has to be true. If my dad isn't crazy...then it has to be, right? It has to be. No, it can't be real, what am I saying? No one is going to end the world. The prophecy has to be fake, there's no such thing as a prophecy to end the world.

It was just then that it hit me.

Unless...I was the one who could foretell the prophecy...and not only would I be the one to foretell it, but I could also fulfill it. If no one else will end it, I have to. There's no other choice. If I don't, not only will those three think my dad is crazy, but they'll also never forgive me and think *I'm* crazy. But that can't be the only reason I have to do this, no. The reason I have to do this is...I can't let my father down.

I have to be the one to end the world.

Author Notes / Afterword

Hello, thank you so much for reading Visions of a Lotus Flower Volume 1. It has been a tough journey getting everything set up, but after finally completing it…I can confidently say it was worth it. I have so many ideas for Owari and Miya's journey; it's hard not to keep writing. I have left clues in Volume 1 for what's to come in the future, so it would be exciting to see everyone speculate. My writing is always improving, so the next volume will be even better. Thank you to saika and Keiko Nakamura for providing the beautiful artwork.

I wonder what Owari will do next...

GEM

○

Thank you to GEM for giving me the opportunity to illustrate the cover. I am glad to be a part of your novel. Feel free to contact me here: saika.work8@gmail.com

saika/Japanese Illustrator

Made in the USA
Las Vegas, NV
01 December 2022